D1022243

PRESUMED PUZZLED

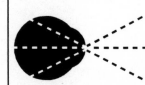

This Large Print Book carries the
Seal of Approval of N.A.V.H.

MYSTERY

PRESUMED PUZZLED

PARNELL HALL

THORNDIKE PRESS

A part of Gale, Cengage Learning

Farmington Hills, Mich • San Francisco • New York • Waterville, Maine
Meriden, Conn • Mason, Ohio • Chicago

GALE
CENGAGE Learning®

LIBRARY OF CONGRESS CATALOGING-IN-PUBLICATION DATA

Names: Hall, Parnell, author.
Title: Presumed puzzled : a Puzzle Lady mystery / By Parnell Hall.
Description: Waterville, Maine : Thorndike Press, 2016. | ©2015 | Series: Thorndike Press large print mystery
Identifiers: LCCN 2016000764 | ISBN 9781410488169 (hardcover) | ISBN 1410488160 (hardcover)
Subjects: LCSH: Felton, Cora (Fictitious character)—Fiction. | Crossword puzzle makers—Fiction. | Women detectives—Fiction. | Murder—Investigation—Fiction. | Large type books. | GSAFD: Mystery fiction.
Classification: LCC PS3558.A37327 P74 2016b | DDC 813/.54—dc23
LC record available at http://lccn.loc.gov/2016000764

Published in 2016 by arrangement with St. Martin's Press, LLC

Printed in Mexico
2 3 4 5 6 7 20 19 18 17 16

For Erle Stanley Gardner,
who got it right

GUILTY!

I do not possess the talent to create the puzzles needed for this book. I therefore plead guilty to incompetence, and throw myself on the mercy of better cruciverbalists than I.

Luckily, Will Shortz, crossword puzzle editor for *The New York Times* and author of his own very successful series of crossword puzzle and Sudoku books, rushed to my defense and contributed the necessary Sudoku puzzles.

Not to be outdone, noted *New York Times* constructor Fred Piscop offered the court Defense Exhibits A, B, and C in the form of the missing crossword puzzles.

And before I could speak up and sabotage their fine work, American Crossword Puzzle Champion Ellen Ripstein edited the puzzles and saved me from my own mistakes.

Without the help of these three people, I

would probably be heading directly to jail.
  I rest my case.

CHAPTER 1

"I need a client."

"Of course you need a client," Cora said. "You're a lawyer. Lawyers need clients."

Becky Baldwin shook her head. Her long blond hair fell in her face. That was the problem with looking like a supermodel. It sometimes got in the way of her practice. People assumed that anyone who looked like she'd be at home on a catwalk couldn't know anything about the law. They would be wrong. Becky had a keen legal mind and a particularly adept courtroom manner. In choosing a lawyer, they could hardly do better. "No. I said, 'client.' Not 'clients.' 'Client.' Singular. As in one. As in any client at all."

"You don't have a client?"

"I haven't had a client in weeks. I come into the office, I sit and stare at the wall."

"You want me to find you a client?"

"Exactly."

"Where do you expect me to find one?"

"Well, I wouldn't try staring at the wall." Becky tipped back in her desk chair. "You got it easy. You sit in your cozy office at home and make up a crossword puzzle for your daily column, which probably takes you a good forty-five minutes, then lay around all day counting your royalties from your book deals and watching the residuals from your TV ads roll in."

Becky had that half right. Cora Felton was the Puzzle Lady, whose smiling face graced the nationally syndicated crossword column and who pitched Granville Grains breakfast cereal to schoolchildren in a series of TV commercials, but she didn't spend forty-five minutes a day creating crossword puzzles. She actually didn't spend any. Cora couldn't construct a crossword puzzle if her life depended on it. Her niece, Sherry Carter, was the true Puzzle Lady and wrote Cora's daily column. Of course, Becky didn't know that. She was one of the few people who knew Cora couldn't solve crossword puzzles but still thought she created them.

"I don't know what I can do," Cora said.

"Can't you go out and kill someone? Then I can defend you from a murder rap."

"I don't think I'm gonna do that."

"Why not? You've done it before."

"No, I haven't."

"I've defended you on a couple of murder raps."

"Yeah, but I didn't do them."

"Right, and I got you off anyway. Which proves I can do it."

"You got me off because I uncovered the guilty party."

"Well, you had to. You were innocent."

"Exactly."

"No, not exactly. It would be a lot easier if you actually did it. We'll know what all the facts are. Nothing will surprise us."

"But I'll be guilty."

"So what? You're presumed innocent. That's the law. You can come into court in a blood-drenched pantsuit holding the severed head of the victim and the jurors have to presume that you're innocent or they're unacceptable and can't sit on the jury."

"I don't have a pantsuit," Cora said.

"Well, so much for that idea."

"Becky, I don't think you quite understand how this works. The lawyer gets a client. The client *hires* the attorney. Then the attorney *hires* the private investigator to go out and do the investigating. The attorney doesn't hire the investigator to go out and bring her a client."

"I don't want to hire you to bring me a

11

client. I can't pay you. I can barely pay my rent, and the dump I live in is dirt cheap."

"Becky, I sympathize, but I'm not going to kill anyone just because you need the work."

"Spoilsport. All right, then, why don't you get divorced?"

"I'm not married."

"I'm broad-minded. I won't hold that against you."

"You're really desperate?"

"You have no idea."

Cora sighed. "I'll see what I can do."

CHAPTER 2

Bakerhaven Police Chief Dale Harper was amused. "You want me to shill for Becky Baldwin?"

"Of course not, Chief."

"That's what it sounds like. Throw some business her way. Like you want me to go out and arrest someone so she can defend him."

"That's nothing," Cora said. "She wants me to go out and shoot someone so she can defend *me.*"

"That's a better idea. And it keeps me out of trouble."

"Oh, yeah? You don't wanna *know* the kind of trouble you're gonna have if you try to arrest me."

"You'll never take me alive, copper!" Harper said, in his best Jimmy Cagney voice. "Isn't that a line from one of those old movies you're always quoting?"

In Cora's opinion the chief's best Jimmy

Cagney voice was none too good. "And now *you're* quoting them, Chief."

"Damned if I'm not," Harper said. "Look, it's not that I don't like Becky Baldwin. But I can't solicit business for her. It's not ethical. I pick up a guy for speeding, say, 'Here's how it works. You can go in front of the judge, pay a fine, get points on your license. But if you wanna play it smart, I know this lawyer can get it knocked down to a simple fine, no points. And you don't want points on your license, because you get too many and you lose your license and then good luck trying to get it back.' See what I mean? Not entirely kosher."

"Well, when you put it like that."

"The best I can do is advise 'em of their rights. Tell 'em they have the right to an attorney. If they ask me are there any attorneys in town, I can say, 'Yeah, Becky Baldwin.' That's not hyping, shilling, or pimping for her. It's not even a recommendation. It's just answering the damn question."

"Well, can you tell *me*?"

"Huh?"

"We're friends. If I call you up, 'Hi, Chief, how's it goin', arrest anyone today?' "

"Maybe."

"What do you mean, maybe?"

"There's a question of privacy."

"Privacy? It's not a privacy issue. When someone gets booked it's a matter of record."

"You don't get booked for a speeding ticket."

"Forget the speeding ticket! You wanna recommend Becky defend a speeder, fine. I'm talkin' robbery, rape, and murder."

"We don't get so many of those."

"You get your share."

"It's no secret. I don't have to tip you off. If something like that happens, the whole town knows."

"Are you trying to be annoying, Chief? You're always calling me up with stuff that doesn't make the papers. Break-ins, burglaries, car thefts, stuff like that."

"Those are crimes, not perpetrators. They're not something I've arrested someone for. They're open cases where I value your input. You're really good at getting to the bottom of things."

It was true. As bad as Cora was at crossword puzzles, she was good at crime. In the past she had helped Chief Harper with several homicides. Not to mention several lesser offenses.

"Chief —"

Harper put up his hand. "Cora. We're

friends. I'll help you if I can. You scratch my back, I'll scratch yours. That's what friends do. You want me to do you a favor, I certainly will. Just like I know you'd do a favor for me."

Uh oh.

Cora suddenly had severe misgivings. Something bad was about to happen. She could sense it.

"That's really nice of you, Chief. Becky will appreciate it."

"Yes. And I'm sure she'd do me a favor if she could. But that really wouldn't be ethical. It's not the same as friends helping friends."

"I'm glad to hear it, Chief," Cora said. She hastily got up to go. "Glad I stopped in."

"I'm glad you did, too," Chief Harper said. "There's something I wanted to ask you. The selectmen are organizing a benefit to help the local police department. I was wondering if —"

Kill me now, Cora thought.

CHAPTER 3

Jennifer raced across the front lawn and hurled herself headfirst onto the monkey bars.

"She's going to knock her teeth out," Cora said.

Sherry Carter laughed. "Well, aren't you the nervous Nellie. I thought it was the mother who was supposed to be overprotective, not the great-aunt."

"Well, you don't have to bend over backwards in the opposite direction," Cora said. "It's a wonder the kid got to be as old as she is. How old is she?"

"She's three."

"Three going on sixteen. I tell you, that kid's ready to start dating, and, trust me, she'll choose the most undesirable boys."

"Now, now, Cora. Just because you did doesn't mean she will."

"I chose wonderful boys. It's husbands

where I had a problem. So did you, as I recall."

Sherry's first husband, Dennis, had been a disaster. He was the reason for the whole Puzzle Lady facade. Cora had never forgiven him for it.

"I'm batting five hundred," Sherry said. "A damn sight better than your average."

"Yeah. I'm below the Mendoza line. You don't have to rub it in."

"The Mendoza line?"

"He had a lifetime two hundred batting average. How can you create puzzles and not know that?" Cora pointed. "Look what she's doing now!"

Jennifer was hanging upside down by her knees from a high bar.

"Relax. She's fine."

"What are you going to tell Aaron when he gets home and finds out she fell on her head?"

"I'll tell him you weren't watching her."

"Sherry Carter, what did I ever do to you?"

"You know what you did to me. You come out here, you want me to construct a crossword puzzle."

"*I* don't want you to construct a crossword puzzle. *Chief Harper* wants you to construct a crossword puzzle."

"Maybe I'm wrong, but doesn't Chief Harper want *you* to construct a crossword puzzle?"

"I can't do it."

"My point exactly."

"You knew I couldn't do it when you got me into this mess. You knew you were always going to have to construct the crossword puzzles for me. Now, do you want to keep doing that, or do you want to tell people I'm a big fake, it's a hollow charade, and let the whole Puzzle Lady franchise crash and burn, along with the sizable income that allows us to pay for this nice Connecticut property, including the comfortable two-story addition? Or do you think we can make it on Aaron's salary alone?"

Sherry's husband was a reporter for the *Bakerhaven Gazette*.

"Aaron works hard."

"So do you. Oh, no, you don't. You retired from teaching preschool to handle the less demanding but far more lucrative job of writing crossword puzzles. Every now and then you'll be called upon to create an extra one to keep up the facade, but that seems a small price to pay for the cash cow that is the Puzzle Lady franchise."

Jennifer had untangled herself from her upside-down position and was traversing the upper rungs of the monkey bars like a spider.

"You should have a video camera," Cora said.

"We do. I just have so much footage of her climbing the monkey bars already. Now, what is it Chief Harper wants, exactly?"

"A crossword puzzle extolling the virtues of the police department."

"You've got to be kidding."

"That's what he wants."

"Can it be funny?"

"How can it possibly be funny?"

"You don't write my column. *Anything* can be funny. I just need a short poem about the police."

" 'Our cops are tops.' "

"Not that short."

" 'Bakerhaven's finest —' "

"Whoa, whoa, whoa!" Sherry said. "I'm not doing a Sunday puzzle here. We're talking fifteen by fifteen. 'Bakerhaven's finest' is more than fifteen letters itself. I need lines nine or ten letters long."

"Now I have to write the poem for you?"

"Unless you trust me to do it."

"Now why does that sound like a threat?"

"It's not a threat. I'm just warning you what you're going to get."

"There's a poem. 'Ain't no threat, it's

what you're gonna get.' "

"Never mind. I'll do it myself."

"That's probably wise," Cora said.

"You couldn't just make him a Sudoku?"

"I made him a Sudoku." Cora reached in her floppy drawstring purse, pulled it out, and held it up for Sherry.

6						8		
4		3						
9	7	2			3	6		
7	6							
2				6				
			4	8			5	
	4		3		7			9
	9	7	1		4		6	8
			5			1		7

"You expect me to solve this?" Sherry said.

"No. I know you're not able to. Which is why I don't taunt you with it and make fun of you. Because I'm a nice person who appreciates the congenial working relationship that is the basis of the Puzzle Lady franchise."

Sherry said something that could hardly be considered congenial.

"My, my," Cora said. "It's a good thing Jennifer's way over there on the monkey bars."

"So? You gonna solve this or not?"

Cora dug in her purse for the solution. "Here you go."

6	1	5	2	7	9	8	3	4
4	8	3	6	1	5	9	7	2
9	7	2	8	4	3	6	1	5
7	6	4	5	9	1	2	8	3
2	5	8	7	3	6	4	9	1
1	3	9	4	8	2	7	5	6
8	4	1	3	6	7	5	2	9
5	9	7	1	2	4	3	6	8
3	2	6	9	5	8	1	4	7

Sherry scanned the solution grid. "So what's it mean?"

Cora shrugged. "Nothing. It's just numbers. Which is why Chief Harper wasn't thrilled. Which is why I need a puzzle."

Sherry looked up from the Sudoku. "You showed this to me just to point out I couldn't do it?"

"No. To point out I tried to save you. I don't bring you puzzles just to torture you. Only when I can't get out of it."

"You couldn't have sicced the chief on Harvey Beerbaum?"

Harvey was Bakerhaven's other resident cruciverbalist. He, like Becky, knew Cora couldn't solve puzzles. When the police wanted help with one, she often passed the honor on to him.

"I tried. It's for charity. It's not so much the puzzle they want as the Puzzle Lady name."

"Wonderful."

Cora stuck the Sudoku in her purse, looked back at the monkey bars.

Jennifer was climbing down headfirst. Somehow she made it seem logical.

"Anything else I can do for you?" Sherry said sarcastically.

Cora cocked her head. "You wouldn't

have a client for Becky Baldwin, would
you?"

CHAPTER 4

"You seeing someone?"

Stephanie's eyes widened in outrage. "You can't ask her that. This is a woman in your life. You have feelings for her. You know it, she knows it, I know it. Asking her if she's seeing someone is like saying you don't have feelings for her. And we all know that isn't true."

"Just making conversation," Crowley said.

Stephanie rolled her eyes. "Men!"

"I'm not seeing anyone I'm in imminent danger of marrying, if that's what you mean," Cora said.

"That should cover a lot of territory, with your track record," Crowley said.

Stephanie hit him with a couch cushion. "You get worse and worse. Cora will be sorry she came."

"I'm glad you invited me," Cora said. "Sherry's a good cook, but her daughter's three, and she's all over the place. There's only so much I can take."

"Stephanie's a good cook," Crowley said.

"She must be, if she's cooking right now and she's in here."

"In here" was the living room of Crowley's Greenwich Village apartment. The Jimi Hendrix poster on the wall might have seemed out of place for a beefy NYPD homicide sergeant but made sense after Cora met Stephanie. A thin woman in a madras smock with long flaxen hair and no makeup, Crowley's girlfriend was a refugee from the sixties whose Bleecker Street tapestry shop had evolved into its present incarnation as a fabric store.

"It's all in the timing," Stephanie said. "And the preparation. You get everything ready to go and it cooks itself. Didn't you ever cook?"

"Not if I could help it. I used to make macaroni. Of course, it comes in a box and takes seven minutes."

"So you know how to boil water."

"Absolutely," Cora said. "It's what attracted Frank."

"Frank?"

"My third husband. I think he was third. There's a gray area, what with the annulments."

Crowley got up and poured himself a

26

bourbon. "It doesn't bother you that I'm drinking?"

"Not a bit. I like a man who drinks. Not that I have to get 'em drunk, usually. Maybe a few shy types."

"It doesn't bother you that you're not drinking?"

"No, the one thing has nothing to do with the other."

"Are you in AA?" Stephanie said.

Cora shook her head. "Not my style. If I don't drink, it's because I don't want to drink, not because a bunch of people I don't know pressured me into feeling guilty about it."

"That's not what AA does," Stephanie said.

"Are you in it?"

"No, but I know enough people who are."

"I thought it was anonymous."

"It is. That doesn't mean people can't tell you they're in it."

"Yeah, well, I quit drinking on my own. I quit smoking on my own. And when I quit dating, it will be entirely on my own, and not because someone asked me in a supportive way if I was seeing someone."

"Oho!" Stephanie said. "What a way to turn the conversation around with a devastating zinger. Well done!"

"Sounds like you don't need any help," Crowley said.

"Unless you know someone who needs the services of a Bakerhaven lawyer."

"Becky Baldwin needs work? I don't know why. That girl is damn good."

"There's not a lot of business in Bakerhaven."

"She should move to New York."

"Hey!" Cora said. "Don't deprive me of my one source of entertainment. Doing Becky's legwork is what keeps me sane."

"I thought there *is* no legwork," Crowley said.

"I rest my case."

CHAPTER 5

Aaron Grant flew Jennifer around the living room like an airplane, with Buddy the toy poodle nipping at his heels, while Sherry showed Cora the crossword puzzle.

Across

1 Like much tribal lore

5 Word with bug or misty

9 Emeril catchword

12 Dollars and cents

14 It's nothing to a tennis player

15 Harbor workhorses

16 START OF A MESSAGE
18 Zoning measure
19 Has no truth to it
20 Ottawa's prov.
21 Depot posting, familiarly
22 Not the real thing: Abbr.
24 Rapunzel's abundance
26 Do some KP work
29 Figs.
31 Soccer fan's cry
32 "Slippery" trees
33 MORE OF THE MESSAGE
38 Org. with a much-cited journal
39 Explorer aided by Sacagawea
40 Nanki-_____ ("The Mikado" role)
41 MORE OF THE MESSAGE
44 See 12-Across
45 TV channels 2-13
46 Source of fatback
48 Sax type
49 Gets the better of
53 Gimlet or screwdriver
55 Ken of "thirtysomething"
56 MLB playoffs mo.
58 Walks off with
62 Fonda's beekeeper role
63 END OF THE MESSAGE
65 _____ the lily (overdo it)
66 For the asking
67 Recruit's negative

31

68 "_____ give you the shirt off his back!"
69 Burpee bagful
70 Moments, briefly

Down

1 Prefix with potent
2 Down-under bounders
3 Bartlett's abbr.
4 Soup legumes
5 Brother of Peyton
6 John's "Two Virgins" collaborator
7 Decathlon segment
8 Wipes out
9 See 12-Across
10 See eye to eye
11 Some teachers' degs.
13 Tom Sawyer's assent
15 Fez feature
17 Beef or pork cut
23 Vacancy sign
25 Keebler baker
26 Potpie spheroids
27 "Blondie" boy
28 Online read, for short
30 Cut into cordwood
34 "Shut up!"
35 Stone for many Libras
36 Blog comment

"Okay, here it is," Sherry said. "I just couldn't do a long support-our-hard-working-police-department-to-whom-we-owe-an-enormous-debt-of-gratitude message."

"Right," Cora said. "It doesn't fit in the grid."

"It's not the length of the answer I'm talking about, it's the tone," Sherry said. "I can't do a sickly sweet appreciation. I'm not cut out for it, and neither is the Puzzle Lady. Puzzle Lady puzzles have a little edge to them, a little barb, a little playful quality. That's what makes them Puzzle Lady puzzles and not the puzzles of anybody else."

"What are you buttering me up for?"

"What do you mean?"

"There's something about this puzzle I'm not going to like that you're trying to prepare me for."

"Absolutely not. I think you're going to love it. But —"

"What?"

Sherry made a face. "Chief Harper may not."

"Let me see."

Cora took the puzzle and read: " 'No one likes lazy flops. So get it up for the cops.' "

"What do you think?"

"I love it. Aggressive, insulting, erotically suggestive, and homosexual to boot. Chief Harper will be thrilled."

"Sorry. I was getting punchy."

"It's wonderful. He'll never ask me again."

"Show her the other clues," Aaron said, as the Jennifer airplane glided by.

"There's more?" Cora said.

"Just a clarification," Sherry said.

"Yeah," Aaron said. "She's more specific about what she wants you to get up."

"Is it a four-letter word?" Cora said.

"One of them is."

"Sherry, how bad is this?"

"Not bad at all. The answers are 'cash,'

'money,' 'dough,' 'bucks.' "

"You missed 'shekels.' "

"It didn't fit the grid."

The phone rang.

"Saved by the bell," Cora said. "I don't care who that is, just so it gets me out of the conversation." She took the receiver off the hook, wandered back into the living room on the long cord. "Hello?"

"Cora? Chief Harper."

"I'm on it, Chief. As a matter of fact, I've come up with the most wonderful homo-erotic puzzle."

"What?"

"Relax. You'll love it, and contributions will double."

"I don't know what you're talking about," Harper said, "but you asked me to call if I got anything. You want this tip or not?"

"What is it?"

"A missing persons report."

"You got a missing persons report?"

"No, I got a *report* of a missing person. Only, I *don't* have a report of a missing person, because you can't have a report of a missing person until they've been missing twenty-four hours."

"Chief, either you're not making any sense, or I'm still stuck in puzzle mode. What are you talking about?"

"You know Paula Martindale?"

"I play bridge with Paula Martindale."

"Her husband's missing."

"You're kidding!"

"He didn't come home from work last night."

"No?"

"No. He works in the city. Odds are he hooked up with some woman, stayed over.

Not going to win him Husband of the Week, but not unprecedented."

"Yeah," Cora said. "Hmmm."

"What's the matter?"

"I don't understand."

"What?"

"Why are you calling me?"

"You wanted me to tip you off."

"That's not a client. It's not even a case."

"No, but it could be."

"What do you mean?"

"The guy's missing. If he turns up, fine. If he turns up dead, and it's a homicide, the wife's always the most likely suspect."

"She came to you," Cora said.

"Which would be a good move if she just killed her husband and was trying to escape the blame."

"Whoa, whoa, Chief. You're getting way ahead of yourself. Nobody killed her husband. It's not even a missing persons report."

"That's right. Like I say, I can't investigate it."

"Right."

"But you can."

"Huh?"

"You're a friend of hers. You can call her up, say, 'I heard Roger's missing; look, this is not unprecedented, I've been married before, this happens all the time, I know you're probably going nuts, let me come talk to you, you'll see it's not so bad.' "

"You really have a devious mind, you know it?"

"What do you mean by that?"

"You want me to pump this woman under the guise of friendship."

"What's devious about that? It's just good cop–bad cop without the bad cop."

"I'm glad that doesn't strike you as devious."

"Come on, Cora. Give it a whack. You'll be doing me a favor, then if anything does come of it, you'll have the inside track with Becky Baldwin."

"Speaking of favors?"

"What?"

"You're going to love your puzzle."

CHAPTER 6

The Martindale residence was a two-story white frame house with black shutters on Glenwood Street. Though fashionably unpretentious on the outside, the house was garish on the inside. Having played bridge with Paula Martindale, Cora was not surprised. Paula was an aggressive player, with a tendency to overbid her hand and blame her partner. Cora didn't like playing with her, but she had joined the game a year ago when one of the regulars dropped out. The other regulars were First Selectman Iris Cooper and Judy Douglas Knauer, the real estate agent. Judy had brokered the deal on the Martindales' rental, and Paula had asked her about bridge. It hadn't occurred to Judy that her unusual interest in asking a virtual stranger indicated an obsessive personality probably not harmonious to the group. Cora couldn't stand being partnered with the woman and was not at all surprised to find her living room overdecorated with paintings, vases, wall hangings, even a freestanding bronze statue of a boy on a dolphin.

The woman herself was garish in an overtly sexual way, a predatory man-eater, arrogantly flaunting her youth in Cora's face. Not that she was any spring chicken herself, just enough Cora's junior to be able to accentuate the difference with dress and makeup enough to relegate Cora to out-of-the-running, over-the-hill noncom. Paula exuded confidence. It was in fact her most obnoxious trait. She knew that she was right and everyone else was wrong, but she would condescend to point out the error of their ways.

Cora was surprised when Paula met her at the door. She seemed hesitant, confused, shaken, entirely out of character.

"So," she sniffed, ushering Cora in the door, "Chief Harper wouldn't come himself."

"It's not an official missing persons report yet."

"Yes, yes. Chief Harper went over all that. Those ridiculous rules people follow like drones. You ought to be able to use common sense. There's a big difference between some crack-addict baby-daddy who never

40

comes home anyway and a respectable, hardworking man who'd never failed to come home in his life."

"There certainly should be some flexibility," Cora said. "My ex-husband Melvin was missing more often than not. Filing a report would have been foolish. But that shouldn't taint the pool."

Paula was in no mood to hear about Melvin. "What?" she said irritably.

"Why don't you tell me what happened."

"What do you mean, what happened? He didn't come home."

"Yesterday?"

"Yes, of course, yesterday."

"The last time you saw him was yesterday morning?"

"Yes. After breakfast when he left for work."

"What time was that?"

"Seven thirty, seven forty-five. What difference does it make?"

"So you haven't seen him in over twenty-four hours."

"That's what *I* said. Then Chief Harper calls his office and they say he hasn't been in today, and he asks them if he was in yesterday, and they say, yes, he was in all day. So he says that means he was last seen five o'clock yesterday afternoon, which means it hasn't been twenty-four hours yet."

"Makes sense."

"To who? Some lazy police officer trying to get out of doing his job? So what if someone else saw him within twenty-four hours. *I* haven't seen him within twenty-four hours. And where's he get off taking someone's word for it on the phone anyway? That wouldn't stand up in court."

"Yes, but you're not *in* court," Cora said. "And nothing you can say is going to force Chief Harper to do anything until it's been twenty-four hours, so you might as well let nature take its course."

"Is that what you came out here for? To take Chief Harper's side?"

"No. He thought I might be able to help. Which was really his way of helping. Since legally he wasn't able to help any other way."

"You're talking in circles," Paula said. "This is not a question of semantics. This is a question of getting my husband back. What are you going to do about that?"

"I don't know what I can do about it, because I don't know the facts. If you could channel all the energy you're spending on anger into doing something constructive, maybe we can figure something out."

"Yeah, like that's really going to help."

Cora didn't think it would, either. The

42

most constructive thing she could think of was strangling the woman. She hesitated, then approached the next subject delicately. "Have you considered the possibility he might have stayed overnight with someone?"

"Not unless he was held against his will. In which case we're talking about an abduction, not just a missing person. Why doesn't anyone understand that?"

"He couldn't have just stayed with another woman?"

"Absolutely not! My husband was incredibly devoted. He called me every day from work just to make sure everything was all right."

"Did he call you yesterday?"

"Of course he did."

"What time was that?"

"Around three o'clock, same as usual."

"Did you mention that to Chief Harper?"

"Why?"

"Well, when you told him you hadn't seen your husband in twenty-four hours, you had heard from him since then."

"What difference does that make? He's missing, I'm worried, but everyone's so concerned about time. I'm afraid something's happened to him. If he could come home he would; obviously, he's being held against his will."

"Have you had any unusual phone calls? Anything that might be the prelude to a ransom demand?"

"No, I haven't. Which doesn't mean nothing's wrong."

"Nothing in the mailbox? Nothing slipped under your door?"

"No, nothing like that . . . Oh, there was one thing out of the ordinary. Chief Harper wasn't impressed." She snorted. "Of course, he wasn't impressed with anything."

"Something out of the ordinary?"

"Yes."

"What was that?"

"Oh. Here. Now, where was it?" Paula pawed through the magazines on the coffee table. "Ah, here we are."

She handed Cora a piece of paper.

It was a crossword puzzle.

Across

1 Group with "turf"

5 Up to it

9 Lacking skill in

14 Creme-filled treat

15 Place for a peephole

16 Like an eremite

17 START OF A MESSAGE
19 Cheek muscle, for short
20 Runway displays
21 Mushrooms-to-be
22 Letters on a tire
23 Buttonhole, essentially
24 Tough time for a batter
28 MORE OF THE MESSAGE
33 Move stealthily
35 Get hammered
36 Head of a board: Abbr.
37 Aardvark's prey
38 Little Eva's creator
40 "The Censor" of Rome
41 "My turn!"
42 Trendy berry
43 Places with hot rocks
45 MORE OF THE MESSAGE
48 Ms. Midler
49 _____d'oeuvres
50 Source of feta cheese
52 Rhythmic, as a drumbeat
55 Like the lunar surface
60 Be crazy about
61 END OF THE MESSAGE
62 Bruce Wayne's home, e.g.
63 Cry from a sentry
64 Venerated one
65 Signs to heed
66 Underdogs may beat them

67 Crammer's worry

Down

1 "An expensive way of playing marbles," to G. K. Chesterton
2 Blueprint datum
3 Brooklyn pros
4 One of a black-clad subculture
5 South-of-the-border signoff
6 '90s European war zone
7 Arcing tennis shots
8 Bard's preposition
9 March 17 instrument
10 Parcels out
11 In a sullen mood
12 Pot starter
13 Shirts with slogans
18 Tutu-clad dancer in "Fantasia"
21 Places to schuss
23 Lay away
24 Reserved in manner
25 Techspeak, e.g.
26 "The Jungle" author Sinclair
27 The Ozarks, e.g.: Abbr.
29 Stiff-upper-lip sort
30 "Not possible"
31 Subtly suggest
32 Wild West loop
34 Armed guard

39 Greek T's
40 Snooker stick
42 Penitent ones
44 Launders money for, perhaps
46 "Monster" Oscar winner Charlize
47 Usher in
51 Rolling Stones drummer Charlie
52 Hunter's garb, for short
53 Genesis figure
54 Ready to serve
55 Scrap in 2000 election news
56 Put out
57 Paella need
58 Grandson of 53-Down
59 Door ding, say
61 "_____ dat?"

CHAPTER 7

Cora slammed the crossword down on Chief Harper's desk. "You forgot to mention this!"

Harper looked up from his paper. "Oh? What is that?"

"As if you didn't know. It's a crossword puzzle. It's Paula Martindale's crossword puzzle. It is the crossword puzzle you neglected to mention before you sent me out there, because you knew if you did I wouldn't go. It's the crossword puzzle you let me lead with my chin and walk right into because I didn't know it was coming."

"Oh. That crossword puzzle."

"I'm not in a good mood, Chief. You have any break in the case yet?"

"What case?"

"The Roger Martindale case."

"It's not a case yet. It's not even a missing persons."

"It's gonna be in a minute. And it's gonna

49

take a whole damn task force to find your scattered remains."

"Did you solve it yet?"

Cora nearly gagged. "No, I did *not* solve it yet. And I'm not *going* to solve it. You're going to take it to *Harvey Beerbaum* to solve. Which is what I've told you to do with *any* unsolved puzzle you encounter in the course of your investigations."

"Well, that's the thing," Chief Harper said calmly. "This isn't an investigation."

"Harvey doesn't know that!" Cora exploded. "Harvey doesn't care. He'll be happy you asked him."

"I'm sure you're right. In the event this becomes a case, I will certainly ask him."

"Fine," Cora said. She picked up the crossword, folded it, and shoved it into her floppy drawstring purse.

"What are you doing?" Harper said.

"I'm taking away this offending crossword puzzle that you're not interested in."

"I'm not interested in it yet. Of course, if this becomes a case I'll expect it to be solved."

"I may have gotten rid of it by then."

"You're planning on throwing it away?"

"Why not?"

"It could be evidence."

"Of what? You can't have evidence without

a case, Chief. I guess I'm stuck with it. Don't worry. Luckily, Sherry has a shredder."

"Now look," Harper said. "Why don't you leave the puzzle here? If the guy doesn't show up and it becomes a missing persons case, I'll have Harvey Beerbaum solve it."

"That would be the way to play it," Cora said. "Only you didn't want to do that."

"I beg your pardon?"

"Paula Martindale gave you the puzzle. You wanted to take it and have Harvey solve it, but you couldn't, not as long as you were claiming there was no case. So what do you do? You leave the puzzle there and send your good friend Cora out to blunder her way into it. And Paula will give the puzzle to me and I'll bring it to you. And you can have it without evincing the slightest interest in it or acknowledging there might be a case."

"That sounds a lot better than the husband barging into my office demanding to know why I'm stealing his crossword puzzle."

"So you thought of that?"

"Of course I thought of that. I'm a policeman. I can't go around exceeding my authority and butting into people's business. If I acted on the report of every wife who was having trouble with her husband —"

Harper put up his hand. "That is not to disparage women or imply in any way, shape, or form their complaints are not valid."

"Oh, for Christ's sake, Chief," Cora said. "I'm not quoting you, and you're not running for office. You abused our friendship to get the crossword puzzle and I don't appreciate it. Let's move on. You want the damn thing, have Dan run off a copy. If it turns into anything, you can have Harvey solve it. And I'll have a copy of my own. Because the one thing that is *not* happening here is you are not finding out the crossword puzzle means something but you can't tell me because Ratface doesn't want Becky Baldwin to know about it."

"That's not going to happen," Harper said.

"Oh, yeah? Suppose Roger Martindale really was abducted? Suppose Becky winds up defending whoever Ratface picks as the kidnapper?"

"Stop calling Henry Firth 'Ratface.' "

"I will when he stops looking like a rat. How'd a guy like that ever wind up county prosecutor anyway?"

Harper ignored her, picked up the phone. "Hey, Dan, come here a minute."

Bakerhaven's young officer came in the

door. It occurred to Cora he wasn't so young anymore, a sobering thought. Yet he still had that boyish eagerness. And he'd always been a big Puzzle Lady fan.

"What's up, Chief?"

"Cora brought in a puzzle. Can you run off a copy for me?"

"Sure. Where'd you get this, Cora?"

"Paula Martindale. Her husband's missing."

"And this is a ransom demand? He's not even listed as missing, Chief."

"He's not officially missing," Harper said. "It hasn't been twenty-four hours. And it's not a ransom demand. At least, as far as we know. Cora hasn't solved it yet."

"She hasn't solved it for you, Chief," Dan said. "But I bet she has in her head. Right, Cora? She can just glance at it and figure out what it must be."

"You give me way too much credit, Dan. I only got this thing because the chief thinks it's important."

"Oh? Why is that, Chief?"

Harper rubbed his forehead. "Dan. Please. I don't think it's important. I'm just covering all the bases in case it might be important. Which isn't likely."

"Yeah, right, Chief," Cora said. "Be sure

53

and call me up if you get any more leads that aren't likely."

CHAPTER 8

Cora found Sherry preparing a roast for dinner. The new addition on the house had a kitchen, but Sherry did a lot of her cooking in the old. Jennifer was just as happy in the living room with Buddy as she was in her new playroom, particularly now that she was old enough to have the run of the house. The three-year-old and the dog would go whooping through the breezeway that connected the old and the new, race up the stairs, jump on every bed, pelt down the stairs, and come swooping back. It was a game of which they never seemed to tire.

Cora flopped down at the kitchen table, dug in her drawstring purse, pulled out the folded paper. "Got something for you."

"Don't tell me," Sherry said. "Chief Harper hated it."

"Hated what?"

"The puzzle."

"Oh. I didn't give it to him."

"*You* rejected it? I thought you were going to go with it."

"I am. I just forgot."

"Forgot? How could you forget?"

"Something came up." Cora unfolded the crossword puzzle.

"What's this?"

"Paula Martindale found this at her house. It's what Chief Harper sent me to get. Of course, he couldn't tell me that because he knew I wouldn't go. Anyway, we went a few rounds about it and he's got a copy to take to Harvey Beerbaum and I've got this copy to bring to you. Though that's not how I phrased it to him."

"You want me to solve this for you?"

Cora suggested something else Sherry could do with the crossword puzzle.

"That's not the way to get me to help you," Sherry said.

"Sorry. Everyone's giving me a hard time. Chief Harper tricks me into going out to Paula's house, I have to hear her whine for half an hour because her husband's gone, then she whips out the crossword puzzle the chief knew about and wanted all along, and I realize I'm being taken advantage of, and used, and made a fool of, plus I'm stuck with a crossword puzzle I can't solve. And I gotta know what it says before Harvey Beerbaum solves it and Harper wants to know what it means. So if you can take any of that stress off my back, I would be eternally grateful."

Sherry washed her hands in the sink, dried them on a dish towel. "Gimme."

Cora passed over the puzzle.

Sherry retrieved a pencil from a drawer Cora wouldn't have known contained pencils, sat at the kitchen table, and attacked the puzzle.

"Is it a ransom demand?" Cora said.

Sherry shushed her. "You do see I'm only half done?"

"Is it *half* a ransom demand?"

Sherry finished the puzzle.

Cora snatched it up, read the theme entry. " 'Let this be a stop sign. Don't touch what's mine.' "

Sherry looked at Cora. "Chief Harper's gonna want to know about that."

"Yeah," Cora said.

"Aren't you going to tell him?"

"He's got a copy of the puzzle. He can always have Harvey solve it."

"He doesn't know it's important."

"Who says it's important? I'm certainly not going to go rushing down to the police station like *I* think it's important."

" 'As if.' "

"Huh?"

" '*As if* I think it's important.' "

"Give me a break. Like anyone thinks I care about grammar."

" '*As if* anyone thinks.' "

Cora suggested an activity Sherry could enjoy alone. Luckily, Jennifer and Buddy were in another part of the house.

Cora snatched up the solved puzzle and stomped back to her room. She flung herself down on the bed, grabbed the remote, and snapped on the TV. Some god-awful game show was on. Cora didn't even bother to change the channel. She picked up the puzzle, moodily studied the solution.

Let this be
A stop sign
Don't touch
What's mine

Yeah, that was going to light a fire under the chief.

It was barely an hour later when he called to summon her to the station.

Chapter 9

Cora skidded to a stop in front of the police station, stomped up the steps, pushed open the door.

Dan Finley was busy on the phone. He waved her on toward Harper's office.

Cora found the chief on the phone. He saw her, slammed it down. "Well, you certainly took your time getting here."

"Sorry, Chief," Cora said sarcastically. "I didn't realize it was urgent. Please forgive me."

"It's been over twenty-four hours. Roger Martindale is officially a missing person. Dan's on the phone trying to trace his car."

"How's he doing that?"

"He's covering every garage within the vicinity of Martindale's office looking for any tan Chrysler not picked up in over twenty-four hours."

"What if it's a monthly rental?"

"That will be easier. The license will be

on record."

"Dan's doing this alone?"

"NYPD's helping him. It shouldn't take long."

"I take it you don't need me to man the phone," Cora said ironically.

"Harvey solved the puzzle. I think you'll find it interesting."

"You don't think I solved the puzzle?"

"No, I think you did. But if you want to pretend you're not interested I have a copy of Harvey's solved puzzle for you."

"You called me in here to look at a puzzle that's already solved?"

"I called you in here because the solution is: 'Let this be a stop sign. Don't touch what's mine.' That seemed pretty significant in light of the situation. At least, it does to me. I'd be delighted to have you point out the error in my deductions."

"How about I point out the error in your deduction that I'm going to do that?"

Dan Finley burst in the door. "Got it, Chief!"

"You found the car?"

"Yes and no."

"Dan!" Chief Harper and Cora snapped the word out together. It was hard to tell who sounded more impatient.

"I found out where it *was*. It was picked

up over an hour ago."

"By the guy who left it?"

"By the guy with the claim ticket. The garage man seemed miffed I might want more than that."

"You call his wife yet?"

"No, I came to tell you."

Harper consulted a paper on his desk, picked up the phone, punched in a number. He let it ring several times and hung up.

"Now *she's* missing. You say he picked up his car an hour ago?"

"Closer to two."

Harper nodded. "Think I'll take a ride out there."

"Why?" Cora said.

"Find out what happened."

"Of course," Cora said. "When he was lost, you couldn't care less. Now that he's found, you can't wait to investigate."

"A guy disappeared long enough to get listed as a missing person. I wanna make sure he understands we don't appreciate that. He'd better have a good explanation, or there's gonna be hell to pay. It's not the same as filing a false police report — I'm not sure exactly what it is — but I don't like it, and I want to be damn sure he knows it."

"This I gotta see," Cora said.

Harper looked at her. "Are you serious?"

"Absolutely. I want to see if you really are going to tear him a new one, or if you're just acting tough in front of Dan."

"Thanks. I think I can handle this myself."

"Nice try, Chief. After using me as a cat's paw, you're not going to deprive me of the fun stuff."

Cora followed Chief Harper out to the Martindale house.

Two cars were parked out front.

"Looks like he's home," Cora said.

"Looks like they both are. Maybe he's just too busy explaining to answer the phone."

As they went up the walk, Cora said, "Look."

"What?"

"The front door's open. You wanna ring the bell or walk in?"

"Ring the bell."

"Killjoy. How about both at once?"

Before Harper could stop her Cora rang the bell and pushed the door further open as chimes sounded in the house.

"Damn it," Harper said, following her in.

Paula Martindale stumbled into the foyer. Her eyes were wide, frantic.

A carving knife in her hand dripped blood.

She looked at Cora, then at Chief Harper, then back at Cora again. She appeared utterly overwhelmed. "Something happened to Roger!"

"Put down the knife," Harper said.

Paula looked at the knife in her hand, seemed to see it for the first time. Instead of dropping it, she raised it like a dagger.

Chief Harper drew his gun.

Cora stepped in front of him, grabbed Paula's arm.

Paula tried to pull away.

Cora twisted her arm.

The knife clattered to the floor.

Cora grabbed Paula in a bear hug, held her tight.

Chief Harper pushed by them into the living room.

Cora wrestled Paula to the living room door.

Roger Martindale lay in the middle of the white plush carpet.

His chest had been hacked open with a carving knife.

There was blood everywhere.

CHAPTER 10

"I didn't do it."

"Who asked you?"

Paula stared at Becky Baldwin. "Don't you want to know I'm innocent?"

"They're all innocent," Becky said. "It's a rule of law. You're presumed innocent until proven guilty."

"I'm not talking about rules of law. I'm telling you a fact. The fact is, I didn't do it."

"I want you to stop saying that."

"Why?"

"Because I don't want you to say anything. You have the right to remain silent. Use it. If the police ask you a question, you say, 'My lawyer told me not to talk to you,' or 'I refuse to answer on advice of counsel,' or however you want to phrase it. Just don't answer the damn question. You tell 'em you didn't do it, you've answered a question for 'em, and it becomes that much easier for them to get you to answer another."

"But —"

"And stop thinking. *You* don't have to plan your defense. *I* do. You have to talk to *me*. Answer the questions *I* ask you. And *only* the questions I ask you. Because I don't want to compromise your defense by having you swear to something I know isn't true."

"Fine. What do you want me to do?"

"I want you to shut the hell up. I want you to not try to account for the fact you were found in the house with your dead husband holding a blood-stained carving knife."

"I just picked it up —"

Becky put her hand over her mouth. "Are you dumb? Do you not hear what I say? I tell you to not account for the carving knife, you start accounting for the carving knife. I understand. You're upset. You've had a traumatic experience. I'm going to have a doctor look at you and he's going to declare you in no shape to answer questions."

"How do you know he'll do that?"

"Because he has to live in this town, and I can make his life a living hell. Don't worry about things you can't control. Because you can't. You are not in charge. You are relieved of responsibility. You have placed yourself in my hands, and I am acting in your best interests. It is not necessary for you to

66

control everything that I do. Nor is it desirable. Your best course of action right now is none. Sit down, shut up, do as you are told."

"But —"

"Shut up and listen. You've been arrested for murder. Your husband is dead. A wife is always the most likely killer. When she's clutching a bloody knife, the likelihood escalates. The police are not apt to be looking for anyone else. As if that weren't bad enough, he didn't come home last night, you were hysterical and reported to the police. He's been missing for twenty-four hours. The next time he shows up he's lying on your living room floor in a pool of blood, and you're holding the knife. You better have a pretty good explanation."

"I thought you didn't want me to talk."

"I don't want you to talk to the police. Eventually, you're going to have to talk to me. And you're probably going to have to talk to a jury."

"Jury?"

"What did you think they do with killers, slap them on the wrist? Short of someone confessing to this crime, you're it. I'll give you the best defense I can, but there's some things I need to know. Chief Harper called you to say he'd located your husband. You didn't answer the phone, which is why he went out there. Where were you when he called?"

"I'd rather not say."

"It's not a case of personal preference. You *have* to say."

"Where I was has nothing to do with anything."

"Are you kidding me? Your husband was out with another woman. He came home and you jumped all over him, demanded to know where he'd been. You didn't like his answers and he didn't like your questions. You wouldn't let up, and he slapped you around."

"You trying to get me off on self-defense?"

"I must say it crossed my mind."

"Forget it. It's one thing to want to run my defense. When you start pleading me out, you're through."

"You start trying to run your own defense, *you're* through. Self-defense is not pleading you out. Self-defense is one of many *strategies* that may be employed in attempting to get a jury to bring back a verdict of not guilty. The operative words are 'not guilty.' Pleading you out means agreeing you *are* guilty of a lesser charge, like involuntary manslaughter or assault with a deadly kitchen implement."

Paula scowled. "Are you *trying* to get me

to fire you?"

"Yes!" Becky said. "I happen to desperately need the work, but the damage my reputation will take for mounting a ludicrous defense for a moronic murder client isn't worth it. If you're going to be that much of a jerk, hire someone else."

Paula looked at her hard for a moment, then shrugged. "Fine, play it your way. I'm not going to tell you where I was, but I'm not going to tell the police, either. So leave it at that and move on."

Becky took a deep breath, considered, reached a decision. "Okay. Have it your way. This afternoon after work your husband picked up the car. He didn't *go* to work, but he picked it up the same time as if he had. He got in the car and drove home, which I assume would take between an hour and an hour and a half."

"So?"

"That would put him at your house at six thirty. Assuming he left the garage at five o'clock. What happened when he got there?"

"I wasn't there."

"Where were you?"

Paula said nothing, set her lips in a firm line.

"I've never been married to a man who stayed out all night," Becky said. "But I can imagine. You're waiting for the guy to get home. Suddenly, you up and leave. That's a tough one to sell to a jury. Even if you say where you went. If you don't, then it's impossible. But have it your way. You weren't there when he got home. What happened when *you* got home?"

"I walked into the living room. There he was on the rug. I couldn't believe it. The rug is white. Pure white. I took such care with that rug. To keep it clean. It stood out. The red splatters."

"What did you do?"

"I was stunned. I just stared at him. And then I saw his chest heave. A slight movement. Like he was breathing. I rushed to him. Knelt down. A knife was sticking out of his stomach. Not his chest. His stomach. I thought, Maybe that's it. Maybe that's why he's still alive. It hadn't hit a vital organ. Stabbed in the belly, not in the heart. I grabbed the knife, jerked it out. The blood oozed out. From where the knife had been. I realized that's what I had seen. Not the chest heaving. It was the seeping blood.

"I heard a noise from the front door. I had no idea who it was. I didn't even know *what* it was. I stood up, stumbled in that direction. I went out in the foyer and there was the police."

CHAPTER 11

Becky came out of the interrogation room.

Cora was waiting to pounce. "What did she say?"

"She didn't do it."

"Gee, that's a shock. What did she say about where she was?"

"I can't tell you."

"Damn it, Becky —"

"I can't tell you because I don't know. She wouldn't say."

"You're her lawyer."

"I pointed that out."

"You should have let me go in there."

"I can't have a confidential conversation in the presence of a third person. You know that."

"You really think she was going to say something you don't want to reveal?"

"She might."

"Like what?"

"Like she killed her husband."

"I thought you said she didn't."

"That's certainly my opinion. I can't count on prosecutor Henry Firth being that broad-minded."

"So what's her story?"

"She came back from wherever the hell she was, walked in, and found him dead. The knife was in the body. She thought he was still breathing and tried to revive him."

"That's it?"

"That's it. You and Chief Harper walk in to find her in an unenviable position."

"But —"

"But what?"

"That's no story at all."

"I quite agree. And that's where you come in."

"You want me to talk to her?"

"You can't talk to her."

"Why not?"

"She's in police custody."

"You talked to her."

"I'm her lawyer. They're not catering to her social schedule."

"So you get me in there."

"I can't."

"Why not?"

"I told you. You can't talk to her with me in the room. The things she says to you while I'm in the room are not a confidential communication."

"So get me in there and leave me alone."

"I can't."

"Are you trying to be annoying?"

"No, but I can't say I'm not enjoying it. It's the only thing I am enjoying about this case. I got a client who couldn't look guiltier, who was holding the murder weapon, and won't say where she was at the time of the crime. She doesn't want to talk about it. How do you mount a defense of that?"

"You poke holes in the prosecutor's case."

"What holes? She was caught with the murder weapon. She had blood on her hands. A cliché, and there it is. She actually had blood on her hands."

"Yeah, she was caught red-handed," Cora said. "So, you're giving up?"

"Why? I got a retainer. In a hopeless case. It's a legal gold mine. I can make more losing this case than I can winning a dozen small ones."

"Becky," Cora said irritably.

"Oh. Pissed you off, didn't I? You cranky from quitting smoking?"

"I barely miss it. Well, maybe four or five times a day. It's not an obsession. Are you really throwing in the towel on this one?"

"Don't be silly. I got you. You're going to

win it for me. Come up with the key piece of evidence to demolish the prosecution's case. To prove her guilty, they gotta prove motive, opportunity, and means. Opportunity's there, the means is in her hand. The motive is not. The police assume he had a lover because he didn't come home. She claims it isn't true. She can claim it till she's blue in the face, but it's either wishful thinking or it's a bad lie. If he was having an affair and the police can prove it, she's dead meat."

"You're probably right."

"Which is where you come in."

"What do you want me to do?"

"Find out."

CHAPTER 12

Feldspar Investments had already heard the news. Brokers eager for details descended on the reception desk when Cora announced why she was there. Interest flagged considerably when they realized she was a woman instead of a cop. On the other hand, they felt freer to ask questions.

"It's true, then," a fresh-faced boy with large round steel-rimmed glasses said. "Roger's wife really killed him."

"You must forgive Dawson," the man Cora figured most likely to be Feldspar, if there indeed was one, said. "He's young and eager and dying for some excitement. He thought it would be like *Wolf of Wall Street*. He keeps waiting for the strippers."

"It's not true Roger's wife killed him," Cora said. "It's true he's dead, and the police are holding her for questioning. The police always question the wife in a case like that, but I wouldn't read too much into it."

"Has she been charged?"

"Not to my knowledge."

"Are you working for her?"

"I'm working for her attorney."

"She has a lawyer?" the young broker named Dawson said.

"She'd be a fool not to. Now, I assume you want to help. Have the police talked to you?"

"Absolutely," the possible Feldspar said. "They were here first thing this morning. They were very interested in what time Roger left work. When I told them he hadn't been in all day they were considerably less interested."

"What else did they want to know?"

"That was basically it. I think they were concerned with what time he would have gotten home. Why does that matter? From what I understand, his wife was found at the scene of the crime."

"With blood all over her," Dawson said. "I hear she was covered with blood."

"He wasn't in all day yesterday?"

"That's right. I suppose he could have popped in and popped out again, but Pam would have seen him."

"And I didn't," the receptionist said. She

was chewing gum and had a pencil stuck in her hair. A computer on a stand was next to her desk. Clearly, she hadn't been hired for her social graces alone. "And I would have noticed. I remember thinking it strange he hadn't been in."

"When he was here, who did he hang out with?"

Dawson seemed amused. "Hang out? This is not a social club. We work here."

"Yes, yes," one of the other brokers said. "You'll get your brownie points, Dawson. She means, who did he go out to lunch with? That would be Brinkman."

"Which one of you is Brinkman?"

"He must be in his office. Show her, Dawson."

Brinkman was on the phone when Cora came in. He put up his hand, finished his conversation, which had something to do with stocks, hung up the phone, and said, "Yes?"

"It's about Roger Martindale."

"Oh. Terrible thing."

"You two were friends?"

"I wouldn't say friends. We're closer to the same age, occasionally go out to lunch."

"You see him yesterday?"

"He didn't come in."

"Talk to him on the phone?"

"Can't say as I did."

"Where'd you think he was?"

"What do you mean?"

"When he didn't come in."

"I don't know. I didn't think about it."

"If you did."

"He got sick. That's the usual reason. People call in sick."

"Did he call in sick?"

"Well, he wouldn't have called me. He'd have called Pam at reception. And she wouldn't have told me. She'd have told Feldspar."

"So there is a Feldspar."

"Of course."

"The police called yesterday. Checking up when he left the day before. You heard about that?"

"Yeah."

"So you knew he wasn't home sick. Where'd you think he was then?"

"I have no idea."

Cora smiled. "Come on, Brinkman. You're buddies. You go out, you shoot the breeze, talk turns to women, some girl in the mailroom with obvious attributes, you get the impression if he wound up somewhere after work you wouldn't have far to look."

"No, nothing like that."

"What'd you guys talk about?"

"Work."

"You got to be kidding me."

"It's what we do."

"Yeah, so you don't want to talk about it. . . . You talk about the Yankees. You talk about the Knicks. You talk about women. You ever have lunch in a strip club?"

"No!"

"Really? There's enough of them around here. I would think by the law of averages you'd blunder into one of them."

"No, we didn't. It wasn't like that at all."

"What was it like? Come on, Brinkman. I'm trying to find out who killed Roger. If there's some woman he might have been with the night he stayed out, I need to know."

"I'd like to help." Brinkman shook his head. "I just don't know anything."

CHAPTER 13

Crowley looked up from his desk. "Oh, hi, Cora. Good to see you. You tell Stephanie you were stopping by?"

"Do I have to?"

"No, I was just asking if you did."

"No, I came to see you."

"I figured that, since you're here. This business or social?"

"If it was social I'd have called Stephanie."

"Would you now."

"No, I just said that because you asked if I had." Cora flopped into a chair. "I'm getting old, Crowley. Old and tired and not up to my job."

"That doesn't sound like you."

"I don't want it to sound like me. Things have been frustrating lately."

"Are you hinting at something?"

"I'm not eager to mess up your life."

"You never are."

"Yeah." Cora took a breath, blew it out. "You know that case Becky was looking for?"

"Yeah."

"She found it."

"Oh?"

Cora gave Crowley a rundown of the situation.

Crowley was amused. "A client holding out on her attorney. Not an entirely unique situation. At least in terms of detective fiction. Didn't Perry Mason's clients always hold out on him?"

"They usually lied to him. With disastrous results."

"Did you point that out to the client?"

"Becky won't let me talk to her."

"That must be frustrating."

"You have no idea."

"So what do you need?"

"I gotta find out where he was the past twenty-four hours. Not the *past* twenty-four hours. From when he left work the day before yesterday until seven o'clock last night, when he got home and either was or wasn't killed by his wife."

"You talk to his friends at work?"

"Yeah."

"They any help?"

"Not a bit."

81

"Okay. I'll put Perkins on it. See if the guy used a credit card anywhere. If he did, we can nail him. I'll call you if I get anything."

"I don't have a cell phone."

"Oh, right."

"*I'll* call *you* if you get anything."

"How will you know?"

"That's what makes it fun," Cora said.

"You got a picture of the guy?"

"Yeah." Cora showed him.

"Not bad-looking. Probably doesn't look so good now."

"I was there when they found the body."

"Right. Good thing you had a cop with you."

"Tell me about it."

"Okay. Anything else you need?"

"As a matter of fact . . ."

"What?"

"The guy from work Roger hangs out with. Name of Brinkman. I asked him about Roger's outside interests and he said there weren't any."

"Maybe there weren't."

"Yeah, but I got twenty-four hours to account for, and I can't think of a better solution."

"So?"

"I got the impression this guy Brinkman

didn't want to talk to me about it because I'm a woman."

Crowley nodded. "Say no more."

CHAPTER 14

"Okay, Brinkman," Crowley said. "I'm a busy man, I don't want to waste the day with this. Roger might have had a woman on the side. Someone he might have stayed with before he went home and got killed. Now who might that be?"

The stockbroker shrugged helplessly. "I have no idea, Officer. I don't think there was one."

"Fine," Crowley said. "Get your hat and coat."

"What?"

"Actually, it's pretty warm. You can come just like that."

"What are you talking about?"

"You don't want to answer questions so you're going downtown, where I can charge you with obstruction of justice and hold you until someone bails you out or your memory improves."

Brinkman gawked at him, open-mouthed.

Crowley was out ten minutes later.

Cora was sitting on the fender of his car.

"You know that's a police car, lady."

"What'd Brinkman say?"

"Roger had a woman, all right. The guy had no idea who it was, but he knew that he did."

"You get a description?"

Crowley shook his head. "Guy didn't know."

"Think he was telling the truth?"

"Oh, yeah. He tried not telling the truth. It didn't work."

"So Roger had a girlfriend. You think that's where he was during the missing twenty-four hours? With someone he saw after work?"

"Or during work."

"Oh?"

"He used to go for a late lunch, take his time getting back."

"He ever leave work early?"

"Not that he knew. All he knew was Roger had a girlfriend and he didn't want to talk about it."

"Roger didn't want to talk about it?"

"Or this guy Brinkman. But he had no choice."

"And Brinkman thought he might have

been with this girlfriend when he went missing?"

"It was possible. He really didn't know."

"Any indication it might have been someone else?"

"Why do you say that?"

"I don't know. Everything is during the day. He suddenly pulls an overnighter. What's that all about? If it was the same woman, why would he do that? Odds are it's another."

"Well, it's a theory."

"Did you ask him?"

"That question specifically? No, but he had no idea."

"Sometimes you can jog a memory."

Crowley's car phone rang. He reached in the window, scooped it up. "Yeah? . . . Give me that again. . . . Good work, let me know if you get anything else." He hung up the phone. "Got a lead."

"Oh?"

"Roger's Amex. Rented a room in a hotel on Fifty-seventh Street."

"The day before yesterday?"

"No. Half a dozen times in the last two months."

"Not what we want."

"Are you kidding me? It's the missing woman. Who cares what day it is?"

"I do."

"Why?"

"My job is to find out where he was."

"Well, don't be so damn ungrateful. ID-ing the woman's gotta help."

"Yeah. Sorry."

"Let's take a run over there."

"Now?"

"Hey. We're a full-service department. You come for help, you get help."

They drove over, found the hotel. Crowley parked at a fireplug and they went inside. Cora hung back, let Crowley take the lead.

The desk clerk was a middle-aged man with bifocals and a sour expression.

Crowley flopped a shield in front of him. "NYPD. Let's see the register."

The clerk didn't seem impressed. "We're computerized."

"Fine. Call this up. Roger Martindale. Hang on, I'll give you his Amex card." Crowley flipped open his notebook, read the number.

The clerk entered it into the computer. "Yeah, he was here. A few times. All within the last month."

"All single-night rentals?"

"Let's see. Yeah, all one-night."

"You notice who he was with?"

"I don't even know who you're talking about."

"Show him the photo."

Cora dug in her purse, slid the picture on the counter in front of the clerk.

He picked it up, looked at it. Shook his head. "I don't think so," he said, and handed it back to Cora.

His mouth fell open. His face became animated. He pointed at her. "It's you!"

Cora shrunk back from the accusation.

Crowley stared at her in surprise.

"You're the woman on TV! Selling the breakfast cereal! You solve puzzles and help the police!" He pointed again. "Puzzle Lady! That's it! You're the Puzzle Lady!"

"That's me," Cora said. "Now about the picture —"

The clerk wasn't about to be distracted by a picture. He had a goofy grin on his face. "What a week this has been! Last Saturday — you're not going to believe this — last Saturday we had Steven Tyler here! You know, from Aerosmith. And he was on *American Idol* for a while. Sam said it wasn't him, but come on, who looks like him? And he wasn't staying here, just visiting someone, so why couldn't it be him?"

"I'm sure it was," Crowley said. "Now, about Roger Martindale."

The clerk knew nothing about Roger Martindale. Apparently, if the guest wasn't a celebrity, the clerk didn't notice him. Still, he was eager to help, if only to ingratiate himself with the Puzzle Lady.

"Bob might know," he offered, in a sudden flash of inspiration.

"Bob?" Crowley said.

"My replacement. On my days off. Let's see here." He scanned the computer screen. "The fourteenth? What day of the week was that? No, I was on. Here we go. The twenty-third. That would be Bob. He may remember him checking in."

"Got a phone number?"

"No, I don't."

"Got a name?"

"Just Bob. But if you want to see him, he'll be in on Tuesday."

"Yeah," Crowley said. He whipped out his cell phone, punched in a number. "Perkins?"

"Yeah?"

"That hotel on Fifty-seventh Street. I got a desk clerk named Bob."

"What about him?"

"Exactly," Crowley said, and hung up.

CHAPTER 15

"Well, that was unproductive," Cora said as they drove back.

"I'll say. For a moment there I thought he was going to peg *you* as the woman."

"Me, too. I was not amused."

"You just have no sense of humor."

"Oh, yeah? How'd you feel if he pegged you for Martindale?"

"Couldn't happen. You had a photo."

"I could have shown him *your* photo," Cora said. After a pause she added, casually, "No reason Chief Harper needs to know about this."

Crowley nearly swerved into a truck. "Are you kidding me?"

"You're not investigating the case. You did this as a favor."

"I'm a police officer."

"And a very good one. You don't infringe on other officers' territory. You don't horn

in on cases that are outside your jurisdic-
tion."

"Cora —"

"And the guy's a terrible witness. He
couldn't ID the photo. He just looked up
the charge on the computer. Hell, Perkins
did that. You think Chief Harper won't be
tracing credit card charges?"

"So? He'll find out anyway."

"Yeah, but Becky Baldwin won't be pissed
at him for doing it."

Crowley grinned. "You're something, you
know it?" He looked over at her. "So, what
you gonna do now?"

Cora cocked her head. "What'd you have
in mind? Something I have to ask Stephanie
about?"

"I'm going back to the office. I got work.
I mean, what are you going to do with your
case?"

Cora grimaced. "I don't know. It's a dead
end. I guess I'm going back to Bakerhaven."

"You don't want to talk to the other desk
clerk?"

"Bob? I thought he only worked on Tuesday."

"Perkins will find him."

"Nah, I gotta get back."

"Oh," Crowley said. "You expect *me* to
talk to him?"

"Weren't you going to take me?" Cora said.

"Yeah."

"So go without me. I'll leave you the photo."

Cora handed it to him. He stuck it in his pocket, wrenched the wheel, swerved around a garbage truck.

"Is this because I asked you if Stephanie knew you were here?"

"Sergeant Crowley, you have a very suspicious mind."

Crowley dropped Cora off at her car. He was on his way back to the station when Perkins called with the address.

Bob was semi-retired, lived in a rent-stabilized one-bedroom walk-up apartment on East 71st Street. He was watching some reality TV show and wouldn't turn it off. He was deaf, and the volume was loud.

"All right," he said. "What do you want?"

"You're a desk clerk at the hotel on Fifty-seventh Street?" Crowley shouted.

"What?"

Crowley picked up the remote control, pushed the Mute button. "This is a police investigation. If I have to take you downtown so you can hear me, I will. You wanna leave the Mute on, or you wanna take a ride?"

"Well, when you put it that way," Bob said. "What you wanna know?"

Crowley passed over the photo of Roger Martindale.

"I couldn't see this with the sound on?" Bob grumbled. He looked at the photo, looked back up. "What about him?"

"Have you seen him?"

"Sure."

"Where?"

"At the hotel. I checked him in a couple of times."

"Who was with him?"

"He came in alone."

"Send anyone up to his room?"

"It's not that kind of hotel."

"I mean a visitor. Did you send any visitors up to his room?"

"No. No one asked for him."

"Are you sure?" Crowley said.

"I'd remember."

"Why?"

"That's my job."

"You know what days these were?"

"No, but it'll be in the register." Bob cocked his head. "What'd this guy do?"

"He got killed."

Bob's mouth fell open. "In the hotel?"

93

"No. In Connecticut. They've arrested his wife for it. If he was seeing another woman, it would be a motive."

"Can't help you," Bob said. His eyes widened. "Wait a minute! This is the murder, isn't it?"

"What murder?"

"The one in the paper!"

There was a copy of the *New York Post* on the coffee table. Bob grabbed it up, turned the pages.

"Here it is!"

On page 8, under the headline BUTCHER OF BAKERHAVEN, was a picture of Paula Martindale accompanied by a picture of her husband. The pictures were not current, in that Paula was not in jail and her husband was alive. They weren't even recent, just what the *Post* had been able to pull from their archives in time to make the late city edition. Roger looked vaguely like himself, but Paula might have been posing for a perfume ad.

The accompanying article, such as it was, said that Roger had been killed, and Paula had been picked up for questioning. The word "alleged" was used several times. Crowley wondered if it applied to the headline.

"That's it, isn't it? That's the man you

were asking about. I knew he was familiar."

"That's the case," Crowley said. "So you can see how important this is."

"I do, but the facts are the facts. He didn't have a visitor. Of course, anyone in the hotel could have called on him. Anyone who'd rented a room."

"Sounds like a lot of work for Perkins."

"Huh?" Bob said.

"Another officer will have to check reservations. For anyone he might have seen."

"Well, you're on the right track," Bob said.

Crowley frowned. "What do you mean?"

"About it probably being a woman."

"Why do you say that?"

"Both times he checked in, he checked out about two hours later."

Back in the car, Crowley sighed.

Cora wasn't going to be happy.

Bob was too damn good a witness.

He'd have to call it in.

CHAPTER 16

Becky was pissed. "You weren't supposed to be finding evidence for the prosecution."

"I'm just as disappointed in Crowley as you are," Cora said.

"Disappointed, hell. I don't recall hiring Crowley. I thought I hired you."

"You never complained when he came up with things in our favor."

"When has he ever done that?"

"I was generalizing."

On the TV over the bar, Rick Reed was holding forth in front of the police station. Cora and Becky were in the Country Kitchen bar because Becky was ducking Rick Reed. Crowley had told Chief Harper what he and Cora had found; Henry Firth had decided the credit card evidence, plus two eyewitnesses who could place Roger Martindale in hotel rooms rented by the hour, made a strong enough case to go ahead and prosecute; and Rick Reed, Channel 8's clueless on-camera reporter, had been dispatched to harass key figures in the drama with ridiculous questions.

Ordinarily, Becky liked sparring with Rick Reed. She always came off well, and she looked great on camera. But faced with an unlikable defendant and a hopeless case, she just didn't have the heart for it. Besides, she was furious with her own investigator and was afraid it might show.

Becky took a long pull on her glass of scotch. "You do recall why I hired you to get this information?"

"So you'd know what evidence the police might be able to dig up."

"Yes, you know why? Because they don't share that evidence with me. That's why I see no reason to share that evidence with them."

"Come on. There's discovery. They can't spring surprise witnesses on you. They have to give you a list."

"In court," Becky said. "They have to do that *in court.* They don't have to outline their whole case for me before I make a fool of myself on television."

"What's the widow's story?"

"She denies it."

"She denies she killed him?"

"She denies he was having an affair.

'Roger would never do anything like that, it must be something else, whatever he was involved with got him killed.' "

"Like getting married."

"Watch it."

"You ready to let me talk to her now?"

"Oh, now that it's going to trial and you really could wreak havoc with any confidential communications?"

"No, now that it's going to trial and it's a hopeless case. Come on, how much worse could I make it?"

CHAPTER 17

"Cora wants to ask you some questions."

Paula sneered. "Why? Aren't you good enough?"

Becky surveyed her client with distaste. "No, I'm not. The evidence is stacked against you and you're playing coy with your lawyer. You got a chip on your shoulder that's blinding you to everything about the case. You can't accept a given fact when it slaps you in the face. You're in a permanent snit. You're so full of smoldering rage I can't let the TV cameras get within a mile of you or you'll pollute the jury pool. You couldn't do a better job of wrecking the case if you took out a full-page ad in *The New York Times* of yourself holding a bloody butcher knife screaming, 'I did it!' I'd like you to talk to Cora because her career doesn't hinge on getting you off for this crime. She's working for me, and she's not intimidated by what you say."

"Nice speech. I'm sure it makes you feel better. Need I remind you that I'm still in jail? When's my bail hearing? When do you plan on getting me out?"

"How does the next millennium sound?" Cora said.

"Do I have to put up with that?" Paula demanded.

"Absolutely not," Cora said, and got up.

"Cora —"

"Let her go," Paula said. "She's no help anyway."

Cora, who was nearly to the door, turned back. "You want help? Come up with one person who saw you anywhere, besides your house, during that one-hour period when your husband came home and when the chief and I arrived."

"No one saw me," Paula blurted.

"Why not?"

"I was tricked."

"You were tricked?" Cora taunted. "A bright woman like you? How in the world were you tricked?"

"With a crossword puzzle!"

The air went out of Cora as if from a paper bag. "What?"

"A crossword puzzle was left on my door-step."

"I'm ready for the looney bin."

Becky waved at Cora to be quiet. "What in the world are you talking about?"

"See?" Paula said bitterly. "That's why I can't tell you where I was. No one will believe me."

"I can't imagine why not," Cora said. "You're charged with murder. It's the perfect time to make up fairy stories about crossword puzzles."

"Can you tell her to shut up?"

"I thought I did."

"You did. I just didn't do it."

"Damn it," Becky said. "Enough sparring. Let's hear the story. You say a crossword puzzle was left on your doorstep?"

"That's right."

"When?"

"I don't know when. I found it at five thirty."

"In front of your door?"

"Yes. It was a crossword puzzle printed on a sheet of paper."

"Why did that make you go out?"

"I solved it."

"And then you went out?"

"Yes."

"Why?"

"Because of what it said."

"What did it say, why would that make you go out, what in the world does this have to do with your missing husband?" Cora said impatiently. "Come on, girl, don't make your lawyer drag it out of you. What the hell happened?"

Paula glared at Cora for a moment, then seemed to wilt. "There was a message on top of the puzzle. It said, 'If you want to know where your husband is, solve this, drive to the mall, park in the far end of the Walmart parking lot. Don't get out of your car; as soon as you're parked roll down the window. Wait ten minutes, set the puzzle on fire, holding it out the window by one corner. When it's burned, roll up the window and wait for further instructions.' "

"That's what you did?" Becky said.

"Yes."

"What happened?"

"Nothing. I waited for half an hour and nothing happened. I felt like a fool. I figured I'd been tricked. I went home and found my husband."

"What did the puzzle say?"

"It doesn't matter."

"It does if you're going to tell that story."

"You want me to talk?"

"Not in a million years. But if you wind up having to tell that story, I need to know the punch line. What did the puzzle say?"

"Some idiotic rhyme. I can't remember it

exactly."

"What was the gist?"

Paula took a deep breath. "There was another woman."

"Oh?"

"It said Roger was seeing another woman. Which is a vicious lie." Paula started getting worked up. "It couldn't have happened. Roger wasn't seeing anyone. I would not have stood for it. I'd have —" She broke off.

"You'd have what?" Cora said.

"I wouldn't have killed him. He was my husband. I'd have killed *her.*"

"Whoa! Whoa! Whoa!" Becky said. "This is all well and good when it's just us, but it's not the sort of thing I would like you to tell anybody else." She said to Cora, "You see the problem with confidential communications?"

"What?" Paula said.

"You can think those things, but don't utter them. You've made your point. As far as you were concerned, Roger wasn't seeing another woman. That's what you thought then. Now there's the credit card evidence and the eyewitnesses."

"Eyewitnesses to what?" Paula demanded. "Did they see a woman, answer me that. All they can show is he was in a hotel. There's

103

a lot of reasons people go to hotels. I'm sure he was there for another purpose. We have to find out what that purpose was. Which is what you should have been doing in the first place."

"Yeah, right, I'm a bad girl," Cora said. "As I recall we left you out at Walmart with a burning crossword in your hand. Care to elaborate on that?"

"Do I have to listen to this?" Paula said.

"Oh, yeah," Becky said. "And stuff ten times worse. You were lured to the mall by a crossword that said your husband was with a woman."

"Yeah," Paula said. "But the police don't know that."

Becky blinked. Opened her mouth to say something, closed it again.

Cora grinned.

"So," Paula said. "Can you get me out of here?"

Becky sighed. "You're not making it easy."

CHAPTER 18

"You know what I'd like?"

"A different client?"

Becky leaned back in her desk chair. "I meant my second choice. Something practical."

"Such as?" Cora said.

"Okay. The cops have these witnesses you conveniently handed them, they're going to go nuts trying to find the woman he was having an affair with. Here we have the advantage."

"How is that an advantage?"

"We don't *want* to find the woman he was having an affair with. In the first place, we don't believe there *was* a woman he was having an affair with, and even if there was, we'd be very happy if she fell off the face of the earth. Finding her is not a high priority."

"I'm glad to hear it."

"Finding whatever *else* he was using that

hotel room for is. That won't be easy, because the police are undoubtedly swarming all over his office, searching his house, checking his email, and downloading the files from his computer. But we know one thing they don't."

"What?"

"The crossword puzzle. The police don't know about the crossword puzzle. And that's a good thing."

"Because they'd think we were nuts."

"No, because it's a big fat clue. The crossword was printed on a piece of paper. Which means it was probably done on a computer. If we can find that computer, we can know who's masterminding the whole thing."

"You're assuming there *is* a crossword puzzle," Cora said. "Your client's had a day in jail to think up any story she likes. So she makes up a story about a crossword puzzle that lured her out of the house. She realizes she's going to have to produce it, which she can't do, so she makes up this preposterous story about burning it in the mall parking lot. I sincerely hope you are not sending me out there to look for the charred corner of a piece of paper."

"It would be nice."

"And you know what it would prove?

Nothing. You give me *ten minutes* and I'll bring you back the charred corner of a piece of paper."

"I'm not asking you to manufacture evidence."

"Oh, there's a quote! I can see them using that when they name you Lawyer of the Year: 'A pillar of integrity, she is reputed to have said, "I'm not asking you to manufacture evidence." ' "

"On the other hand, if you could find evidence this puzzle existed —"

"I could probably walk on water."

There was a knock on the door.

Becky yelled, "Come in."

The door was pushed open by a dweeby-looking middle-aged man, pasty, pudgy, balding, with unflattering tortoise-shell glasses, just the sort of self-effacing person who normally would have said, "Sorry, am I interrupting?" But he was too agitated. Or, Cora figured, what passed as too agitated for him.

"Is it true?" he demanded.

"Is what true?" Becky said.

"You're representing Paula Martindale?"

"I've been retained as her lawyer."

"How can you *do* that? How can you represent that woman? She killed her husband, and you're going to help her get away with it."

Becky smiled. "That's not the way the legal system works."

"I know the way the legal system works. If you have enough money, you can get away with anything. How much does it cost to get away with murder?"

"Excuse me," Cora said, "but who the hell are you?"

"I'm Ken Jessup. Roger was my friend. And that woman sucked the lifeblood out of him until he was too weak to defend himself, and then she killed him, butchered him like a pig. And she's not denying it. She's just sitting there calmly waiting for you to get the legal system to tell her she's free to go."

"What makes you think she's guilty?" Cora said.

"Give me a break. She was caught with the murder weapon." He pointed his finger at Cora. "*You* caught her. How can you be working for her? Aren't you going to have to testify for the police?"

"They haven't asked me."

"Oh, like they're not gonna? Are you going to testify for the defense? Are you going to lie?"

Becky stepped in front of Cora before she bit the man's head off. "Did you come here just to insult us, or do you want to say something?"

"I hear the police have evidence Roger had business meetings in New York."

"Business meetings?"

"At a hotel. Business meetings at a hotel. This is not unprecedented. Businessmen have business meetings. With clients they don't want coming to their office."

"How do you know this?"

"Roger was my friend."

"Wait a minute," Becky said. "Have you told the police?"

"Why?"

"Why? It undercuts their whole theory of the case. They think Roger was killed for having an affair. You have evidence that he wasn't."

Jessup smiled. "That doesn't matter. She *thought* he was. She killed him because she *thought* he was having an affair. It's just ironic that he wasn't."

"Give me a break," Cora said. "Now you claim he wasn't having an affair, but his wife thought he was. How do you know that?"

"He told me so. He told me he didn't know what to do. His wife thought he was having an affair but he wasn't. He didn't know how to prove it."

"Why didn't he tell her about the business

meetings?" Becky said.

"She'd have thought he was lying. He said if she found out about the hotel, she'd go nuts. She wouldn't listen to reason, there'd be nothing he could say. Even if he brought in the people he'd been having the meetings with and had them swear up and down, she wouldn't have sat still for it one moment. Don't you understand? He said if she found out about the hotel she'd kill him." He paused for breath. "You still want me running to the police?"

Becky frowned.

"See? It's a no-win situation. Just like Roger was in. If I testify for the prosecution, you're screwed. If I don't testify for the prosecution, you're screwed. So I have to ask you again the same question you must be asking yourself."

He shrugged, spread his hands palms up. "Why in the *world* are you defending this woman?"

CHAPTER 19

"Well, what do you think about that?" Becky said.

After all his vitriolic pronouncements, Ken Jessup had bowed himself obsequiously out.

Cora went to the door, opened it, closed it again.

Becky raised her eyebrows in inquiry.

"I don't trust him any further than I can throw him, and that's not very far."

"Any particular reason?"

"Are you kidding me? That is the most ridiculous, convoluted story I've ever heard. It's the type of thing *I* would make up. A tangled tapestry of lies and innuendo that skirts the boundaries of reason just enough so as not to be summarily dismissed."

"God save me from a wordsmith."

"God save me from a *lawyer.* If you were anyone else, we could hatch a neat plan together to frame that son of a bitch. Unfortunately, you're bound by *legal eth-*

ics." Cora rolled her eyes. "Talk about oxy-morons! Anyway, the whole time I'm listening to that guy, I'm not sure if he's trying to get us to call him to the stand or keep him off it."

"It's a moot point if he goes to the cops," Becky pointed out.

"Except they'll have the same decision. Does undermining their evidence of a woman trump his opinion that Paula knew about it and was angry enough to have killed? The more I think about his story, a third possibility seems likely."

"What's that?"

"He didn't know anything at all; he's making it up out of whole cloth."

"Why would he do that?"

"Maybe he's just a nebbishy guy who'd like to be noticed."

"You may be right," Becky said. "How do we find out?"

"You want me to make a play for him?"

"Cora! A pudgy, nebbishy dweeb?"

Cora shrugged. "So was Henry. My second husband. He had other redeeming qualities."

"I don't think I want to know what *they* were."

"Quoth the spinster."

"Spinster!"

"I'm sorry. At what age do you qualify as a spinster?"

"I'll have to look it up. Are you trying to make me angry?"

"No, I'm just frustrated by this whole case. You've seen our client. I don't want to run around finding out if her husband was seeing someone or having business meetings, and I certainly don't wanna put in time looking for a phantom crossword puzzle."

"Too bad," Becky said.

"Why? Because if I don't you're going to fire me?"

"No. Because if you can't come up with something, we're going to trial."

CHAPTER 20

Henry Firth smiled at the jury. Cora, sitting in the first row with Sherry, could practically see his ratty nose twitching, smelling the conviction. A nice guilty verdict would be a big notch in his belt, she thought, mixing metaphors. Not surprisingly, Cora had come up with no last-minute evidence, and the trial was progressing as scheduled.

"Ladies and gentlemen of the jury: The prosecution expects to show that the defendant, Paula Martindale, found out her husband was having an affair. Roger Martindale, who worked in New York City, had been renting a hotel room there for afternoon trysts. This had been going on for a month, and might have gone on longer, had not passion finally gotten the better of him. He was gone for more than twenty-four hours. During that time he was not at home, nor was he at work. His wife reported his absence to the police, and he was subsequently put on the missing persons list shortly before he reappeared. He picked up his car from the garage in New York, just as if he were leaving work, and returned home to his wife. We have no direct evidence of just what was said, only of the result.

"The medical examiner will testify to the fact that Roger Martindale was killed by a stab wound to the chest, one of at least seventeen such stab wounds inflicted on him with a butcher knife. A butcher knife from a carving set in the Martindale kitchen. And where did the police recover this butcher knife? Not from the body of the victim. No, they discovered this butcher knife clutched in the hand of the defendant, Paula Martindale. She staggered from the living room of her house covered in blood. Her husband lay dead on the rug, his body ripped asunder by a brutal attack."

Henry Firth looked over to Becky Baldwin. "The defense may attempt to argue that this was a crime of passion, that, shocked by her husband's infidelity, Paula Martindale killed him in the heat of the moment. Do not be fooled by such tactics. There was no moment. Her husband was gone for twenty-four hours. It's not like she caught him with another woman. No, she suspected he was with another woman and waited for him to come home. She lay in wait and struck him down.

"And what proof is there of this? The butcher knife. From the carving set in her kitchen. Her husband was not killed in the kitchen. Her husband was killed in the living room. Which means that Paula Martindale *brought* the butcher knife *from* the kitchen *into* the living room so that she would have it with her when her husband came home. This is not an act of impulse. This is not a burst of passion. This is a cold-blooded, *premeditated* crime. Premeditated. That is what raises the stakes from manslaughter to *murder.* This was a *premeditated murder.*"

Henry Firth raised his finger. "And forget about self-defense. The defense attorney may argue her client needed to protect herself against a stronger man." He laughed, spread his arms. "Protect herself from *what? She* wasn't in trouble. Her husband wasn't coming home to ask where *she'd* been for the past twenty-four hours. He was sneaking home with his tail between his legs, hoping he wasn't in too much trouble. He wasn't about to instigate a confrontation. He was looking to avoid one. Bad luck for him. His wife was not just angry. She was murderously angry.

"And the other thing about the self-defense theory, that Paula Martindale needed the knife to defend herself because her husband was bigger and stronger: Yes, he was. Roger Martindale lived in Bakerhaven. I'm sure some of you have seen him around town. For those of you who haven't, we will introduce pictures of him as part of our evidence. You will see that he was a big, strong, vital man. If Paula Martindale had brandished a knife, there is no doubt he could have taken it away from her. Clearly, she did not. Clearly, she kept the knife hidden and struck without warning, or she could not have delivered the blow.

"Having delivered that blow, having struck him to the ground, she pounced upon the body in a fury and made sure he was dead with no fewer than sixteen extra thrusts of the knife, plunging it into the chest again, and again, and again, until it, and she, and her husband, were covered in blood — blood that stained her clothes and dripped from her hands until she was discovered by none other than the chief of police himself, still holding the knife."

"Misplaced modifier," Cora muttered under her breath.

Sherry had a narrow escape from a giggle.

"We shall prove all this by competent

117

evidence, and we shall expect a verdict of guilty at your hands."

Henry Firth bowed to the jury and sat down.

Judge Hobbs turned to the defense table. "Ms. Baldwin?"

Becky rose from her seat next to Paula Martindale, strode out in front of the jury. As always, Becky had dressed for court. Her dress, though inexpensive, looked like a million bucks. It showed just enough leg to interest the men on the jury while not raising the ire of the women. Her makeup was understated, subtle. Her blond hair was swept back from her face and pinned discreetly up off her neck.

"I've been listening to the prosecutor's opening statement, and I'd like to talk to you about gaps." She put up her hands. "Not the ones where he buys his clothes; I mean the ones in his case."

There was an amused reaction in the court. Some of the jurors smiled. Henry Firth started to rise, then realized his objection would only point to the remark.

"What are the gaps in his case? They're called witnesses. And what are witnesses? They're people who *saw* things. They're *eye*-witnesses. They're people who can testify to something because they *saw* it with their own *eyes.* Not people who can give you their opinion of what they *think* might have happened based on the circumstantial evidence. That's what it's called. The circumstantial evidence. The circumstances surrounding the crime. The witnesses take a look at that and they say, 'Oh, well, here's what happened.' They're guessing, but they don't *say* they're guessing. They're not presented as, 'Here's so-and-so who's going to take a guess for you'; they're presented as *experts.* A long list of credentials will be cited, their experience will be touted as reasons why we should esteem them and value their opinion. And then, when all of that is done, *they will guess.* With absolute solemnity, just as if they knew what they were talking about.

"Now, taking a look at this case —"

"Well, it's about time," Henry Firth said.

Becky smiled indulgently, looked at the judge. "Your Honor?"

Judge Hobbs, used to such courtroom byplay, said, "Mr. Firth, if you would please control such interjections. Jurors will disregard the prosecutor's remark."

"Thank you, Your Honor," Becky said. "In my opinion, they should probably disregard *all* of his remarks, but I thank you for that one."

"Oh, Your Honor —" Henry Firth began.

"Yes. Ms. Baldwin: If you could also refrain from such asides?"

"Yes, Your Honor." She turned back to the jury. "Actually, I was happy to hear the prosecutor express the opinion that my client was not physically capable of overpowering her husband with a knife. That's certainly my opinion, and I'm glad he shares it. But I must say I am amused by the way he states conjecture as facts." Becky put on a voice, imitated her adversary, " 'The knife was brought in from the kitchen in advance, showing premeditation.' Really? How about: Her husband came home, wanted to peel an apple. He went in the kitchen, grabbed a butcher knife. He went to the front door, was surprised to encounter the men he had just been dealing with. He thought he was free of their clutches and here they were again. They pushed their way in, wrenched the butcher knife from him, and proceeded to hack him to pieces.

"Sound far-fetched? You bet. You know why? Because it's pure conjecture. Just like the one the prosecutor states with so much conviction proves premeditation. Good thing you had him to point that out to you, or you wouldn't have known it. Nor would I. Nor would any other sane person on the

120

face of the earth.

"Has it really come to this? Not just that a man of Henry Firth's stature would think he could get a conviction in a case like this, but that he would even attempt it. What happened? Did he have an open day on his court calendar? Was he bored? Hard up for cases?"

Becky shook her head. "It seems a shame to waste the taxpayers' good money on such an ill-conceived flight of fancy. However, if we must, we must. So let's consider just how stupid it actually is.

"Now then, in this case, you have, by the prosecution's own admission, a husband who suddenly exhibits bizarre behavior such as he has never done before. He fails to come home. Not a unique event in the annals of marriage, but a first for this one. The decedent has never failed to come home before. He could have been late, he could have had car trouble, any number of things could have occurred, but in that case, particularly in this day and age of cell phones, he would have called. 'Honey, I have a flat tire on the Merritt Parkway, I called AAA, they say they'll be here in twenty minutes.' That didn't happen. Did the defendant attempt to call her husband on his cell phone? Indeed, she did. Did she report his absence to the police? Several times. And would they act? No, they did not. Because of an antiquated law that requires twenty-four hours before a person can be declared missing. But that did not stop her from trying.

"Now, I ask you, as reasonable men and women: Are these the acts of a woman who intends to kill her husband? No, they are not. They are the acts of a woman who is concerned for her husband's safety. A concern that turned out to be justified.

"And as for the idea that he was seeing another woman, she didn't believe it then, and she doesn't believe it now. If I may go back to the holes in the prosecutor's story, let us not forget the big one: *Where is this woman?* The prosecution can't produce her. They can't identify her. They can't find anyone who has ever *seen* her. The most they can do is infer that she exists, because it would be nice if the defendant had a *motive* for this crime.

"The defendant is presumed innocent until proven guilty. You all know that. Some of you have read the book. Some of you have seen the movie. But you've all heard of it. *Presumed Innocent.* You have to give her the benefit of the doubt." Becky smiled. "Well, in this case, *what* doubt? There *is* no

122

doubt. The prosecutor would *like* to have you think the defendant killed the decedent because he was having an affair. Well, if wishes were horses. Because that's all they are. Wishes.

"Clearly, her husband was involved in something. Obviously something happened to him in that twenty-four hours before he was killed. Do I know why that killing took place in Bakerhaven? No, I do not. I'm just like the prosecutor. *I don't know.* I can guess just like he does. Just like his, quote 'experts' unquote, are going to. I can tell you that some shady character lured Paula Martindale out of the house, took her husband home and killed him, so that she would be suspected rather than him, but I'm *guessing.* Just like the prosecution.

"But you can't be swayed by guesses. You can't be swayed by mine, *and* you can't be swayed by *theirs.* You have to judge the evidence. And if there *is* none, or if what little there is can be explained by a reasonable presumption other than guilt — or at least as reasonable as the prosecution's absurd presumption that it could possibly *show* guilt — you must find the defendant not guilty."

Becky smiled at the jury.

"Don't worry. It won't be hard."

CHAPTER 21

"For once I wish I worked for the *New York Post,*" Aaron said.

"Post!" Jennifer proclaimed happily. She had taken to echoing the ends of sentences, often to her parents' regret.

"Why?" Cora said in between bites of Sherry's osso buco. The family was eating in the old living room in front of the TV, a habit they'd never broken.

"Are you kidding me?" Aaron said. "It would make the front page. Instead of bothering with trivialities like facts, we could sit around all day trying to outdo their HEADLESS BODY IN TOPLESS BAR headline."

"Never do it," Cora said. "That's a classic."

"How about HOT LAWYER KICKS ASS?"

"Ass!"

Cora nearly choked on her veal. "Pretty

good." She jerked her thumb at Jennifer. "But it's nothing without your Greek chorus."

"I would love to make something about the fact Becky Baldwin looks like a Gap dancer and made a crack about the prosecutor buying clothes at Gap."

"Hundred bucks if you can fit *that* in a headline," Cora said.

"Oh, no," Sherry said. "Now he'll spend all night trying to do it."

"Do it!"

"Does she know that's two words?" Cora said.

"Words!"

"Want her to explain the rules?" Sherry said. "She's the only one who understands them."

"Bring her into court," Cora said. "Let her echo Ratface."

"Ratface!"

"Is Ratface two words or one?" Cora said.

"One!"

"How about LEGGY LAWYER GAP ZAP?" Aaron said.

"There's nothing about dancing," Sherry said.

"No, but you put pictures of Becky and Ratface on the cover and that sells it."

"Particularly if you can get a shot of Becky

showing a lot of leg," Aaron said.

"Leg!"

"You do know when you get ecstatic about an old girlfriend's physical attributes you're in dangerous territory," Cora said.

"Tory!"

"That's half a word," Cora said.

"I rest my case," Sherry said.

Cora grimaced, shook her head. "No, no, no. If you start spouting courtroom expressions you're just leading him on."

Aaron turned to Cora. "What are you doing now," the young reporter said, changing the subject.

"What do you mean?" Cora asked.

"For Becky? What are you doing for Becky? Aren't you investigating the case for her?"

"I would be, if there were anything to investigate. Now that we're in court, we're counterpunching. The prosecutor's gonna put on his case. Becky's gonna want me to check out any evidence he produces. See if she can blunt the testimony of his witnesses."

"That doesn't sound good," Sherry said.

"What do you mean?"

"Ordinarily, you'd be looking for evidence the defendant was innocent. Or to prove someone else did it. But you're not doing that. It's almost as if you've conceded she's guilty, and you're just looking for mitigating circumstances or some legal technicality. Why aren't you looking for the woman he was having an affair with? Wouldn't that be the normal line of investigation?"

"In the first place, we don't believe there is such a woman. And if we found her, what would you have us do with her? Turn her over to the prosecution? Give them the motive they've been lacking? Or hide her away so the prosecution can't find her? There are penalties for concealing a witness. Some of them are rather harsh. Becky's convinced there was no such woman. It's in our interest to prove that's true. Unfortunately, it's very difficult to prove a negative."

"So what's Becky going to do?" Sherry said.

"I have no idea."

"Will it be interesting at all?"

"Why?"

"I'm going again tomorrow. In the morning, at least. After I drop Jennifer at preschool."

"School!" Jennifer said.

"She really likes school," Cora said.

"What's not to like? A bunch of kids her own age trashing a room."

"Better theirs than ours," Cora said.

"Great. Sit in on court. It'll be fun. Every-one loves a train wreck."

"Is it that bad?" Sherry said.

Cora snorted. "Worse. Becky's really screwed."

"Screwed!"

CHAPTER 22

For his first witness Henry Firth called
Chief Harper, who took the stand and testified to driving out to the Martindales' house
and finding the body.

"And what time was that?" Henry Firth
asked.

"Around seven o'clock at night."

"Was anyone with you at the time?"

"Cora Felton, the private investigator for
the defense."

"Were you there in your official capacity?"

"Yes, I was."

"For what purpose?"

"Paula Martindale had reported her husband missing, and he'd been put on the
missing persons list. In the course of the
police investigation we discovered that
Roger Martindale had left his car overnight
in a garage in New York and had just picked
it up. I called Paula Martindale to report
this and got no answer. I'm a husband. I

have a wife. If I stayed out all night, I imagine my wife would want to talk about it. I figured Roger and his wife might be having quite a conversation and weren't answering the phone, so I decided to take a run out there."

"Why? If he was already home, you didn't need to tell her he'd been found."

"If he was there I wanted to let him know just how the police felt about someone disappearing on a whim long enough to get put on the missing persons list."

"And why did Cora Felton tag along with you?"

"She happened to be in the police station. When Paula Martindale reported her husband hadn't come home, he wasn't gone long enough to be listed as a missing person, so I couldn't act on it. When Paula kept calling, I asked Cora as a favor to go talk to her. Cora had come in to report when we got the call Roger had been found."

"So she went with you?"

"That's right."

"When you got there, what did you find?"

"The front door was ajar. Cora pushed it open and we went in. Moments later the defendant came out of the living room. She was covered in blood and had a large carving knife in her hand."

"What did you do?"

"I told her to drop the knife."

"Did she?"

"Not at first. Not even when I drew my gun. Cora Felton actually had to twist it out of her hand."

"What happened then?"

"Cora restrained her, and I looked in the living room."

"What did you find?"

"The decedent was lying in the middle of the living room rug. His chest had been hacked open, and he wasn't breathing. I immediately called for medical assistance, but it was clear it would not do any good. I called for police assistance, and officers Dan Finley and Sam Brogan arrived on the scene shortly thereafter."

"You asked the defendant what happened?"

"Yes, I did."

"What did she say?"

"She didn't say anything."

"What did you do then?"

"I placed the defendant in custody and held her for questioning."

"Did you advise her of her rights?"

"Yes, I did."

"Did she make a statement?"

"No, she did not. She remained silent and

requested an attorney."

"Thank you, Chief. That's all."

Becky Baldwin stood up, smiled at the chief. "Chief Harper, I believe you testified that the decedent picked up his car from a garage in New York, is that right?"

"Yes, it is."

"But you don't actually know that, do you?"

"Ah, technically, I guess not. I'm relying on the investigation made by Dan Finley, one of my officers. I'm sure he'll be out in a minute, if you want to ask him about it."

"Thank you, I'll do that," Becky said. "No further questions."

"Well, you're actually going to get your opportunity," Henry Firth said. "Call Officer Dan Finley."

Dan Finley looked young on the witness stand. He had a certain eager, boyish quality that was accentuated by its contrast to the solemnity of the court. He had always reminded Cora of a schoolboy doing show-and-tell.

"Is he old enough to vote?" Cora whispered.

"Shhh!" Sherry hissed. She and Cora were in the front row, just behind the defense table. "Judge Hobbs will hear you."

"That old codger? Isn't he deaf?"

He might have been, but the bailiff wasn't. He raised his finger to his lips, shushed Cora. She made a pooh-poohing gesture but complied. After her numerous appearances in court, Cora and the bailiff were friends.

Dan Finley testified to securing the crime scene, dusting for fingerprints, and taking photographs.

"Did you dust the murder weapon for fingerprints?"

"Yes, I did."

"Did you find any?"

"Yes. There were several fingerprints on the handle and even a couple on the blade."

"What did you do with them?"

"I photographed them in place, then lifted the prints and sent the photographs, lifts, and murder weapon to the lab."

"Thank you, Officer Finley. Your witness."

Becky stepped up. "Officer Finley, Chief Harper suggested you were the person to speak to about the decedent picking up his car from the garage. Was this on the same day that he was killed?"

"Yes, it was. I found out Roger Martindale had picked up his car from a garage in New York. I told Chief Harper, and he went out to Martindale's house and found him dead."

"How soon after you told Chief Harper

133

did he go out to the house?"

"Right away."

"Right away?"

"Well, first he tried to call on the phone. When he got no answer, he went right out."

"Cora Felton was with him at the time?"

"That's right."

"You came into his office, where he was talking with Cora Felton, and told him Roger Martindale had picked up his car from the garage?"

"That's right."

"How did you know?"

"What?"

"How did you know he had picked up his car?"

"Oh. Roger had just been put on the missing persons list and I was canvassing for information. I started covering all the garages in the vicinity of the office where he worked, and I got a hit. The garage man told me he'd just picked it up."

"This was on the phone?"

"Yes."

"I see," Becky said. "So you don't know he picked up his car, either."

"I beg your pardon?"

"All you know is someone on the phone said he picked up his car. A nameless, faceless person you never met. You cite his words as gospel: Roger Martindale picked up his car. Tell me, Officer Finley, did your" — Becky made air quotes — " 'police investigation' consist of anything more than making a phone call?"

"I learned it on the phone, yes."

"From a garage attendant?"

"That's right."

"Have you ever met this garage attendant?"

"No, I have not."

Becky nodded, turned away, walked toward the defense table as if she were done with her cross-examination. As Dan Finley started to get up from the stand, she turned back.

"Officer Finley, you say you processed the crime scene?"

"That's right."

"Did you search the body of the decedent?"

"Yes, I did."

"What did you find?"

"His wallet was in his pocket. Along with his identification, including a photo ID. Not that we needed it. We knew Roger Martindale."

"What else was in his pockets?"

"Cigarettes. A few tissues. Small change."

"Was that all?"

"May I consult my notes?"

"Of course."

Dan took out a small notebook, flipped it open. "Let's see. Cigarettes, tissues, small change. A letter he hadn't mailed. An interoffice memo and a small pad of paper."

"Anything else?"

"No, that's it."

"You say a letter he hadn't mailed. How do you know it was a letter he hadn't mailed?"

Dan shrugged. "He still had it."

Laughter rocked the courtroom. Judge Hobbs banged the gavel.

"I mean as opposed to a letter he had received."

"Oh. It was addressed, stamped, sealed, ready to go. As opposed to postmarked, opened. Any of the things you would associate with a letter someone had gotten."

"Who was the letter to?"

"It was a business letter. Paying a bill, I believe."

"You said a notepad?"

"Yes."

"What did he have to write in it, a pen or a pencil?"

"He didn't have either one."

"Oh. That's a little strange, isn't it?"

"Strange?"

"Well, how's he going to write?"

Dan started to answer, stopped, put up his hands. With a good-natured grin he said, "I want to be careful not to say something funny here. I know this is a serious matter. I assume he had a pen or a pencil at his office. He just neglected to take one with him."

"Uh huh. And you say he had cigarettes. What type of lighter?"

"He didn't have a lighter."

"Oh, he had matches?"

"No, he didn't."

"Ah," Becky said. "You assume he had matches at the office also?"

"I really have no idea. I assume his car had a cigarette lighter."

"Oh. Good point," Becky said. "And you found nothing else on the body of any interest?"

"No, I did not."

"Thank you. That's all."

Dan Finley left the stand and Judge Hobbs declared a ten-minute recess.

Becky conferred with Cora at the rail. "I'm not getting anywhere."

"You're doing fine."

"I was until Dan Finley got a laugh."

"Act like *you* got a laugh. The jury will give you credit."

"Are you telling me how to try a case?"

"No, I'm telling you how to do stand-up comedy. Come on, Becky. You're usually good at this stuff. Don't worry. I know what's wrong."

"Really? What?"

Cora leaned in, lowered her voice. "You don't believe in your client and you don't believe in your case."

Becky looked at Cora, deadpanned, "Thanks. I needed that."

CHAPTER 23

When court reconvened, Dr. Barney Nathan took the stand. He did so with confidence. Socially awkward, particularly around Cora Felton since their affair, he was calm and self-assured in court. The medical man was in his element, happy for an opportunity to flaunt his expertise. He rattled off his qualifications matter-of-factly, barely able to conceal how proud he actually was of them.

"Thank you, Doctor," Henry Firth said. "And were you called to a crime scene to examine the body of the decedent, Roger Martindale?"

"Yes, I was."

"Was he living?"

"He was not."

"You pronounced him dead?"

"I did. Without hesitation. He had suffered several lacerations to the chest, a couple of which alone would have caused death, as well as several to the belly. There was extensive loss of blood, far too great for there to be any chance of life."

"Did you subsequently perform an autopsy on the body of Roger Martindale?"

"Yes, I did."

"What were the results of that autopsy?"

"Roger Martindale sustained extensive internal damage. Several of the wounds were in the heart, the aorta was severed, the right ventricle was punctured twice. By 'punctured,' I don't mean a small, clean hole, as with an ice pick. I mean punctured as by a sharp, flat object that delivered a vertical slice."

"You say the wounds were not consistent with a puncture by an ice pick?"

He shook his head. "Not at all. They were consistent with the stabbing of a knife."

"The body was dead when you first examined it?"

"That's right."

"How long had it been dead?"

"Less than an hour. The body had barely begun to cool."

"Thank you, Doctor. And aside from the wounds to the chest, were there any other wounds to the body?"

"There were not."

"No defensive wounds on the hands or

the arms?"

"None."

"So the victim was surprised by the fatal blow?"

"Objection, Your Honor," Becky said. "If the prosecutor is going to testify, I ask that he be sworn."

"Sustained," Judge Hobbs said. "Mr. Firth, you know the proper time to argue your case, and it is not now. Please confine yourself to questioning the witness."

"Yes, Your Honor. I have no further questions."

Becky got up and approached the witness. One of the hazards of practicing in a small town was sometimes you knew the witnesses all too well. Becky's name had once been linked to the doctor's. It was fiction. Cora had created that illusion in order to hide her own fling with the married man. She had done it so effectively that some people still believed it to be true.

Becky smiled at the witness. "Good morning, Dr. Nathan. I have one or two questions regarding your testimony."

"Of course." Barney straightened his bow tie, gave every appearance of being attentive, impartial, fair-minded.

"I believe you stated that you pronounced Roger Martindale dead without hesitation."

"That's right."

"You didn't examine the body, you just walked in and said, 'Oh, yeah, this guy's dead'?"

"Of course not. 'Without hesitation' is just a figure of speech. There was no doubt about it. I examined the body and was quickly able to determine what even a layperson could see. The man was clearly dead."

"And really most sincerely dead?" Becky said.

"Oh, Your Honor," Henry Firth said. "Is defense counsel doing a stand-up routine or questioning the witness?"

"Ms. Baldwin," Judge Hobbs said, "I'm sure I needn't remind you this is no laughing matter."

"I apologize, Your Honor, but I do mean to make a point. About the doctor's rather cavalier attitude in assuming the man was dead."

Judge Hobbs's gavel cut off the doctor's sputtering retort. "That will do. If you wish to make a point, do it by acceptable questions."

"Yes, Your Honor. Dr. Nathan, you used the words 'without hesitation' as a figure of speech?"

"That's right."

"You didn't literally mean without hesitation. You merely meant there was no question as to the matter, is that correct?"

"That's right."

"What other parts of your testimony are false?"

Barney's mouth fell open. "None of my testimony is false!" he said indignantly.

"You said without hesitation, and you didn't actually mean that. If you don't like the word 'false,' what other parts of your testimony did you not actually mean?"

"Objection, Your Honor. Counsel is badgering the witness."

"I think you've made your point, Ms. Baldwin."

"Yes, Your Honor," Becky said. "But surely I have the right to question the testimony of a witness who doesn't mean what he says."

"And you've done that. Unless you have a specific point, move on."

"Yes, Your Honor. Dr. Nathan, you testified that the victim had been killed within an hour of the time you examined the body."

"That's right."

"You base that on the body temperature?"

"For one thing. Also lack of rigor mortis. Skin tone. Coagulation of blood."

"Could it have been longer than an hour?"

"I don't think so. It's not impossible, but

it isn't likely. I examined the body very shortly after death. Probably a half an hour. An hour is a reasonable parameter, but I can't give you an ironclad guarantee."

"Thank you, Doctor. That's a very good answer. I would be inclined to trust your judgment." Becky changed her tack. "I believe you found no defensive wounds?"

"That's right."

"Neither of the hands were cut?"

"No, they were not."

"Is that unusual?"

"I would say so. With so many lacerations to the chest and belly, you would expect to find at least some on the hands and arms."

"A lack of defensive wounds would tend to indicate the decedent did not put up his hands to try to block the fatal blows?"

"That's right," Dr. Nathan said warily. Becky's questions seemed to indicate she was agreeing with everything he said; still, after her previous examination, he couldn't help feeling suspicious he was being led down a garden path.

"That's interesting. Tell me, Doctor, did you look for any contributing cause of death?"

"Contributing?"

"Aside from the lacerations to the chest. From your testimony the lacerations clearly *caused* death. I'm wondering if you found anything else."

"No, I did not."

"Did you test for drugs?"

"Yes, I did."

"What were you looking for?"

"I wasn't looking for anything. I was just being thorough."

"Did you find any drugs present in the body?"

"Nothing significant."

"Nothing significant?"

"No."

"Did you find anything *in*significant?"

"I found the trace of a sedative."

"A trace?"

"Yes."

"How much of a trace?"

"Not enough to be significant. It showed that the decedent had taken a sedative that had time to wear out of his system. Perhaps the day before."

"Which sedative?"

"Ativan."

"Ah. I see. For the benefit of those jurors not on Ativan, how strong is it?"

"Well, it's not a neuroleptic. It's an anti-anxiety drug. A tranquilizer."

"It would calm a person down?"

"Yes, it would."

"Tell me, Doctor, were you Mr. Martindale's physician in his lifetime?"

"Yes, I was."

"Did he have a prescription for Ativan?"

"Not that I know of."

"You never wrote him one?"

"No, I did not."

"Interesting. And in addition to the Ativan, did you find a trace of any other drug?"

"No, I did not."

"How about alcohol? Was there alcohol in his system?"

"Yes, there was."

"Oh, really? How much?"

"The blood alcohol content was point-oh-nine."

"Point-oh-nine?"

"Yes."

"Correct me if I'm wrong, Doctor, but isn't point-oh-*eight* considered legally drunk?"

"I believe so, yes."

"His blood alcohol content was greater than that?"

"Yes."

"So Roger Martindale was legally drunk when he was killed?"

"Yes, he was."

"But you didn't think this was particularly important."

146

"I beg your pardon?"

"You didn't mention it on direct examination."

"I wasn't asked."

"No, you weren't. Did you know you weren't going to be asked?"

"Objection, Your Honor. How is that possibly relevant?"

"Rephrase the question," Judge Hobbs said.

"Were you told by the prosecutor not to mention the blood alcohol level in the victim unless specifically asked about it by the defense?"

"Objection, Your Honor. How is what I may or may not have told this witness possibly relevant?"

"I would tend to agree, Ms. Baldwin."

"Yes, Your Honor. But if the witness *acted* on that suggestion, if he deliberately *withheld* certain facts from his testimony, if there was *in his own mind* the intention *not* to mention something because the prosecutor had told him that he shouldn't, that would certainly be an indication of his bias, and I would have every right to bring it out."

Judge Hobbs sighed. "Yes, you would. Objection overruled."

"No," Dr. Nathan said. "I didn't intend to mention it."

"Uh huh. And was there anything *else* you deliberately withheld from your testimony at the suggestion of the prosecutor?"

Henry Firth nearly knocked over his chair, leaping up to object.

Becky suppressed a smile.

It occurred to her she had pretty well ensured that Dr. Barney Nathan would never ask her out to dinner again.

CHAPTER 24

Sherry picked Jennifer up at preschool with mixed emotions. At one time Sherry had taught preschool. She loved it, but she loved being a mother more. Still, seeing the children playing together in the schoolroom always spurred a tinge of regret.

Jennifer was stacking blocks. She spotted Sherry and sprang up with an excited whoop, knocking the blocks over. "Mommy! Mommy! Mommy!" she cried, ran across the room, and leapt into Sherry's arms.

"How was school?" Sherry said.

"Fine." It was what she always said.

"She had a great day," Alice said. Alice was one of the older teachers, had been there in Sherry's day. The other teacher, Louise, was the third replacement since she'd left. They didn't seem to stick.

"I made a picture!" Jennifer announced.

"She did finger painting," Alice said. "Oc-casionally on the paper, but mostly on her classmates."

Sherry had noticed splotches of color on some of the children. Parents were encouraged to send their kids in clothes that could take a beating.

"It would appear that a bath is in order," Sherry said.

"No bath!" Jennifer said, and laughed hysterically.

"I didn't hear you," Sherry said. "Did you say that you want a bath?"

"No bath!"

"I'm going to have to tickle you until you say 'bath.' Do you want a bath?"

Jennifer giggled. "No bath!"

Alice waved at Sherry and Jennifer as they giggled and "no bath"ed out the door.

Jennifer climbed into the front seat. "I'm a big girl. I don't need a car seat."

"No, you need a bath."

"No bath!"

"What do you want, a bath or a car seat?"

"No bath!"

"Ah, you want a car seat."

"No car seat!"

"Put on your seatbelt and we'll talk about it."

Jennifer snapped on her seatbelt and Sherry drove home.

"All right," Sherry said. "Run upstairs and

turn the water on."

Jennifer ran into the bathroom. Sherry followed, heard the water running in the sink. The water was shut off. Jennifer came out and presented her hands. Most of the yellow and some of the blue had been washed off. Sherry wondered whether more of it was in the sink or on the towel.

The toy poodle, roused from his nap, came scooting around the corner.

"Buddy!" Jennifer squealed, and she and the dog charged down the stairs and bayed through the breezeway.

Sherry caught up with them, as usual, in the living room in the old end of the house. It occurred to her that any remaining finger paint would be a contribution to Cora's quarters and not hers. That was all right. Cora had never once complained about Jennifer-and-Buddy damage.

Sherry left the two of them destroying the living room and went in the kitchen to rustle up something for lunch. Aside from the chicken they were having for dinner, there was very little in the refrigerator. Sherry really did need to do some shopping. She found a can of vegetable soup and a box of macaroni.

The next time Jennifer and Buddy swooped through the living room, Sherry stuck her head in and said, "Soup or macaroni?"

"Macaroni!" Jennifer squealed. Buddy seemed in agreement, and off they went.

Sherry put water on. While she waited for it to boil, she went down the hall to check the email on Cora's computer. Cora handled some of the Puzzle Lady mail herself, but technical questions regarding puzzles, Sherry had to answer. There was none. Only fan letters of the folksy sort Cora could knock off in her sleep.

Sherry went back in the kitchen, where the water was boiling. She dumped in the macaroni, set the timer to beep in seven minutes.

It occurred to her she had some work to do for the crossword column. Sherry did most of her constructing on the computer upstairs, but she spent so much time in Cora's end of the house that she had installed a version of "Crossword Compiler" on Cora's machine. She went back in the office, clicked on the icon, and opened the program.

Sherry was about to set up a grid to work on when she noticed there was a puzzle saved she didn't recall constructing. She frowned at the screen. She didn't recall it at all. Had Cora constructed a puzzle? Sherry wasn't aware of hell freezing over lately, but not only did she not recall the puzzle, some of the clues were ones she would never use.

Across

1 Plaster backing
5 "Bearded" bloom
9 Well-basted
14 "Night" author Wiesel
15 Zippo
16 What nouns and verbs should do

17 START OF A MESSAGE
19 Remote-control craft
20 Bad stretch of time for farmers
21 Puts in a bad light
22 PGA member
23 Male gobblers
24 What honey doesn't easily do
28 MORE OF THE MESSAGE
33 Oil tanker cargoes
35 Price-tag words
36 Internists' org.
37 Wharf pests
38 Focus of a supermarket test
40 Perch for a bighorn
41 Teacher's deg.
42 Longitude word
43 Moocher
45 MORE OF THE MESSAGE
48 Places for altars
49 Native Canadian
50 Anthem contraction
52 Over-the-top fads
55 Leave port
60 In the midst of
61 END OF THE MESSAGE
62 Skier's hangout
63 Go on first
64 Filing aid
65 Locket contents, maybe
66 Adopted son of Claudius

67 Cookiedom's Famous_____

Down

1 More than risqué
2 Banned orchard spray
3 Like Tim Cratchit
4 Cacklers
5 Printing press part
6 Had to reorder
7 Fox hit show, informally
8 Magician's prop
9 Curie and Tussaud
10 Like Shrek
11 Meteorite element
12 Parodied, with "up"
13 Augusta eighteen
18 2-Down target
21 British Conservatives
23 Beta version, e.g.
24 Phillips head, e.g.
25 Where many Goyas hang
26 Finish ahead of
27 Fingers in a lineup, briefly
29 Cause of errors, often
30 Brings in
31 Spin doctor's concern
32 Sources of wisdom
34 Puts on, as a play
39 Stadium near Citi Field

40 Shield wearer

42 Tees off

44 Opening section

46 Bakers' finishing touches

47 Computer network device

51 Prefix with centrism

52 Distiller's ingredient

53 Cupid, by another name

54 Junction point

55 Popeye prop

56 Gumbo need

57 Famous twins' home

58 "Happy motoring" gas brand

59 Hieroglyphic reptiles

61 Took the gold

Rather than clicking to the solution grid, Sherry printed the puzzle. If this was indeed Cora's puzzle, Sherry wanted to check it by solving it.

The timer beeped. Sherry got up, went in the kitchen, drained the macaroni, added cheese and butter, and stirred the mixture into the most wicked child trap imaginable.

She stuck her head out the kitchen door, yelled, "Come and get it!"

An explosion of little feet heralded the arrival of child and dog. A funfest erupted, with macaroni flying in so many directions it would be difficult to tell who had actually eaten more.

Sherry watched in amusement, any thought of Cora's crossword long gone.

CHAPTER 25

After lunch the desk clerk took the stand, identified himself as Harold Brown, and testified that he had worked at the hotel on 57th Street for the last four years.

"Did the decedent, Roger Martindale, ever stay at your hotel?" Henry Firth asked.

"Yes, he did."

"How do you know?"

"I checked him in."

"Personally?"

"Yes."

"How do you know it was him?"

"I recognized him from his picture."

"Do you have the registration book with you?"

"The registration is electronic. I printed out a copy to refer to."

"I ask that the registration printout be marked for identification."

"No objection to marking it for identification, Your Honor," Becky said. "I reserve the right to object to the printout itself as not being the best evidence."

"So ordered," Judge Hobbs said.

The court clerk marked the exhibit.

Henry Firth handed it back to the witness. "Now, Mr. Brown, can you tell me how many times did the decedent stay at your hotel?"

"According to the registration, Roger Martindale checked in six times during the two months before he was killed. On four of those occasions I checked him in myself. Two of the times another clerk was on duty."

"And on the times you checked him in, how long did he stay?"

"He registered for one night."

"And did he stay the night?"

"Objection, Your Honor. How would he know where the decedent spent the night?"

"Could you rephrase the question, Mr. Firth?"

"On the occasions when you registered the decedent, did he check out the same day?"

"Yes, he did."

"How long after he registered did he check out?"

"Between one and two hours."

Henry Firth smiled, spread his arms, and shrugged at the jury, inviting them to share his amusement at how easily he'd gotten around Becky's feeble objection. "Thank you, Mr. Brown. No further questions."

Becky was on her feet. "You say you recognized the decedent when he checked in?" she said breezily.

"That's right."

"Do you recall being questioned in your hotel by Sergeant Crowley of the NYPD in the company of Miss Cora Felton, the Puzzle Lady? I'm sure you do, because you recognized her from television and greeted her effusively. Do you recall that?"

"Yes, I do."

"And Miss Felton showed you a photo of Roger Martindale and asked if he was the man who rented the room and you had no idea. Do you recall that?"

"Yes, but that was before I had a chance to think about it."

"And to see his picture in the papers?"

"Your Honor, that's not a question, it's an argument," Henry Firth said.

"I'll withdraw it," Becky said. "At any rate, you now recognize Roger Martindale as the man who checked in?"

"That's right."

"Did you recognize him when he checked out?"

"I beg your pardon?"

161

"You remember him checking in. Do you remember him checking out?"

"I don't understand the question."

"You say he checked out after one to two hours. Did he come up to the desk, say, 'Hi, I'm checking out, here's my room key, could I have my bill'?"

"Oh."

"Did he do that?"

"I don't remember."

"I didn't think you did. Tell me, Mr. Brown, is it possible to check out without going to the front desk?"

"Of course. You can check out electronically and leave your keys in the room."

"And if Roger Martindale had done that, you wouldn't see him leave."

"No."

"So when you say Roger Martindale checked out, all you really know is that, according to your computer, someone electronically checked out of the room."

"That's right."

"Tell me, Mr. Brown: Is it possible to check out electronically and *stay*?"

"Huh?"

"Well, you don't surrender your key. You can pretty much do as you please. The worst that can happen is you tell a chambermaid, 'No, no, I'm still here,' and she's got other rooms to do, she's not apt to argue with you."

The witness, discombobulated, thought that over. "I suppose."

"Thank you, Mr. Brown. No further questions."

"Any redirect?" Judge Hobbs said.

At the prosecution table, Henry Firth conferred with his trial deputy, obviously over whether to try to repair the damage. He decided not to.

"No, Your Honor. I call Bob Krantz."

The replacement clerk took the stand.

"Your Honor, the witness is someone deaf, so forgive me if I raise my voice."

"We will make allowances," Judge Hobbs said.

In response to some rather loud questions, Bob Krantz testified to the fact he was a part-time clerk at the 57th Street hotel.

"And did you ever see the decedent?"

"Yes, I did."

"Where did you see him?"

"He checked into the hotel on two occasions."

"Are you sure it was him?"

"I never forget a face."

"And did you see him check out again?"

"Yes, I did."

"After how long?"

"The first time, I'm not sure. The second time was an hour and a half."

"Did he come up to the desk and check out?"

"No, he did not."

"Then how do you know he did?"

"I saw him leave."

"And how do you know what time it was?"

"The first time he left it wasn't till later I realized he'd checked out, so I can't tell you exactly what time it was. But I knew he'd only been there a short time. So the second time he checked in, I paid attention. When I saw him leave, I checked the register, saw he'd already checked out. It was an hour and thirty-five minutes after he'd checked in."

"Why did you do that?"

"It's my job."

Henry Firth smiled at Becky Baldwin. "Your witness."

"Thank you," Becky said, much too politely. "Mr. Krantz, did Roger Martindale have a woman with him when he checked in?"

"No, he did not."

"Did any woman ask for him at the desk?"

"No, they did not."

"So all you really know is the time he checked in and the time he checked out.

You don't know what he was doing in that room. In fact, you don't even know he was in that room at all. For all you know, he could have checked in, sat in the hotel bar for an hour and a half, and checked out."

"That would be a damn fool way to spend your money."

"But he could have done it. You have no idea."

"No, ma'am, I don't."

"Thank you. No further questions."

Henry Firth stood up. "Mr. Krantz, you say you don't know if any woman went up to Roger Martindale's room?"

"That's right, I don't."

"During that hour and a half he was there, could one have done so?"

"Sure."

"How could they have done that?"

"They could have been staying in another room. Or they could have walked into the hotel and gone straight to the elevator. I'm only on the desk one day a week. I don't know who checks in when I'm not there. If someone comes in I didn't check in, I don't recognize 'em."

"You didn't recognize anyone then?"

Bob Krantz cocked his head. "Not at the time, no."

A cold chill ran down Cora Felton's spine.

She bit her lip. She should have seen this coming.

"Do you recognize anyone now?"

"Yes, I do."

"You recognize someone here in court who was in that hotel during that hour and a half when the decedent was in that hotel?"

"Yes, I do."

"Who would that be?"

Bob Krantz pointed his finger. "The defendant, Paula Martindale."

Chapter 26

"What did she say?" Cora demanded.

"Outside," Becky said.

"Rick Reed is outside."

"I'm not afraid of Rick Reed."

"What are you going to say?"

"How does 'no comment' sound?"

"At this point, really bad."

"You got a better quote?"

"Are you kidding me?"

Becky pushed her way out of the courthouse. Every reporter within a hundred miles was on the front steps waiting for her reaction. None of them could beat Rick Reed, who shot to her side as if propelled from a cannon.

"Ms. Baldwin. How do you account for the fact your client was in that hotel?"

Becky actually patted him on the face. "Rick, Rick, you got it all wrong. I don't have to account for a thing. The prosecution does. The burden of proof is on them.

They can't do it, so they're staging theatrical surprises. They don't mean anything, but they're trying to steal as much good press as they can before the whole thing collapses in their faces."

Before Rick could ask a follow-up, Becky and Cora pushed by him and down the front steps. They strode down the side street with reporters in pursuit.

"Think they'll try to break into your office?" Cora said.

"Let's find out."

Becky went up the steps to the second floor, unlocked the door, and let Cora in. She locked it behind her and slid the deadbolt.

"Double-locked?" Cora said.

"At least. I was thinking of moving a file cabinet in front of it."

"What did she say?"

"Hang on."

Becky sat down at her desk, jerked open the bottom drawer, pulled out a bottle and a glass, poured herself a shot of scotch.

"Since when did you drink in your office?" Cora said.

"You're surprised this case is driving me to drink? I should get points for not drinking *more.*"

"Are you going to tell me what she said,

or do I have to strangle you?"

"You know what she said. My hopeless case just got worse. My lying, no-good client just handed the prosecutor his motive all tied up in ribbons."

"She followed him?"

"Damn right she did. Little Miss My-husband-wouldn't-do-that knew damn well her husband *would* do that. She's a nosy, snoopy woman, and she suspected him for some time. She followed him to work, she staked out his office, she followed him to the hotel."

"Just that one time, or had she done it before?"

"No, just then."

"Did she see anything? Besides her husband?"

"No, just him."

"What did she do?"

"What do you think she did? Went home and read him the riot act: 'I know what you're doing; if you don't cut it out I'll divorce you and take you to the cleaners.' "

" 'Divorce you and take you to the cleaners' sounds like a euphemism for something."

"It is."

"For what?"

"Kill you."

"That kind of limits your ability to put her on the stand."

"No kidding."

"And why did she withhold this juicy tidbit from her lawyer?"

"She didn't think anyone would ever know."

"They never do."

"They never know?"

"They never *think* anyone will know. This is not an extraordinary client, Becky. They all lie to their lawyers."

"It doesn't always blow up in court."

"No, you kind of hit the jackpot on that one. So that's why she freaked out when her husband went missing. That's why she went to the police."

"I know that. The only thing I don't know is how premeditated this was. Whether she meant to kill him then."

"You're assuming she's guilty."

"Do you think she's innocent?" Becky said.

"She's innocent until proven guilty."

"How much proof do you want?"

"I don't want *any*. I want something that proves her *innocent*."

"Oh, yeah?" Becky said. "Then find me the crossword puzzle. Right now that's the only thing that's gonna help. And what are the odds it even exists?"

"Not good," Cora said. "If you're counting on the miraculous production of a crossword puzzle to save your defense, you are really out of luck. I'd hunt up Ratface and see if you can plead her out."

"She'd never agree to it. And if I did it without her knowledge she'd sue me for malpractice."

"Can you be your own lawyer in a legal malpractice suit?"

"It's not funny, Cora."

"I know. You sure she's telling you the truth? When she says she didn't see anything at the hotel?"

"I'm not sure of anything at this point. If she was lying about it, I wouldn't be at all surprised."

"What did her husband say when she confronted him about the hotel? Confess his sins and swear he'd be a good boy?"

"He denied everything. Claimed the hotel was for when it got too much for him at the office and he had to get away. He wasn't meeting anyone, he just wanted to be alone."

"She wasn't buying that?"

"Would you?"

"Hell, no. It's the type of lie Melvin would

171

try to sell me when he was too lazy to think
up anything better."

CHAPTER 27

Becky Baldwin's face filled the TV screen. "*I* don't have to account for a thing."

Rick Reed's smile was mocking. "That's what Becky Baldwin *said,* but you can imagine what she *thought* when her client was ambushed in court by the surprise testimony of a prosecution witness. Now there is no question her client knew about her husband's matinee excursions in a midtown Manhattan hotel."

"Two different 'her's in the same sentence," Aaron Grant said. "I couldn't get away with that in the paper."

"Rick Reed's a moron," Cora said. "He can get away with anything."

"Is that all it takes?" Aaron said.

"Sure. If you're terminally stupid, no one expects any better."

"I've been going about it all wrong."

Cora and Aaron were watching TV in the living room while Jennifer and Buddy entertained themselves on the floor. Sherry was still in the kitchen cooking dinner. Aaron had offered to help, but Sherry had chased him out. Cora hadn't bothered to offer.

On TV a smiling Henry Firth was playing it modest, pooh-poohing any accolades. "I take no credit for it," he said. "Some cases win themselves. That is not to take away from the fine work our police department has done in this case. And I would like to commend Chief Harper and his force for their efforts in this direction."

"You're talking as if the case were over, Mr. Firth," Rick Reed said. "Aren't you still presenting evidence?"

"Of course," Henry said. "The witness is still on the stand. The judge just granted an adjournment. I would imagine when court resumes tomorrow the matter will be rather quickly resolved."

"You expect the defendant to change her plea?"

"I can't speak for the defense. All I can say is in this particular case I am very happy to be handling the *prosecution.*"

Henry Firth smiled at the camera and walked away.

"That was earlier today," Rick Reed said. "I have tried to get a response from the defense attorney. So far there has been none. Nor has there been a response from the police department, which just received that glowing commendation. I can only wonder what the defense team is doing tonight."

"Isn't that a song from *Camelot*?" Cora said.

"If not, it should be," Aaron said. "I wish there were some way to help Sherry in the kitchen without making it seem like I'm just hungry."

"You're not hungry?"

"I'm starving."

"I can see her point."

"Almost done," Sherry called out the kitchen door.

"No one cares, take your time," Cora called back.

"You got a cruel streak, you know?" Aaron said.

Cora shrugged. "Not according to my divorce lawyers."

"Can't you give me anything exclusive?"

"I got nothing for you," Cora said. "The guy ID'ed our client. It's a kick in the crotch."

"Crotch!"

Aaron sputtered with laughter, shook his

head. "She's getting too smart for her own good."

"Oh, you think she *listens* for naughty words to echo?"

"No," Aaron said. "I think from you she expects it."

Sherry emerged from the kitchen, set plates of chicken, quinoa, and asparagus in front of Cora and Aaron.

Cora pointed at her plate. "What's this?"

"Quinoa."

"Keen-what?"

"Wah."

"You putting me on?"

"You can drop the lowbrow act, Cora, it's just us chickens."

"Oh, yeah? Well, us chickens are winding up on the plate. With the weird-looking rice."

Sherry grabbed a plate for herself, sat down in front of the TV.

The doorbell rang.

"What timing," Cora said.

"I've got it," Aaron said, but he didn't stop cutting his chicken.

"Eat, eat," Sherry said.

She jumped up, went to the front door, and returned with Chief Harper in tow.

"Oh, you're having dinner," Harper said. "I'm sorry."

"I'm not," Aaron said, attacking his chicken. "I'm actually very happy."

"Sit down, Chief," Sherry said. "I'll get you a plate."

"No, no. I'm sorry. I should have called."

"What's up, Chief?" Cora said.

Harper shot a glance at Aaron Grant. "This is off the record."

"Of course it is," Aaron said. "I haven't had a scoop since Clinton was in the White House."

"I just wanted to give you a heads-up. Henry Firth is very happy."

"Yeah, we saw him on TV," Aaron said.

"I'm not talking about that. He's got something else. Something he's not sharing with me."

"And you're here because you want to pay him back," Cora said. "I love it! Spill it, Chief."

"On second thought, I'd better go."

"Hang in there. Can't you take a joke?"

"Don't let Cora drive you away, Chief," Sherry said. "Ever since this case started she's been a big grouch."

"Grouch!"

Harper looked at Jennifer playing on the floor. "Isn't your daughter eating?"

"She is," Cora said. "She plays with the dog and we throw them scraps."

177

"You will not throw my chicken curry on the floor," Sherry said.

"I know. Just the bones," Cora said.

Harper turned to go.

"Come back, I'll be good. We're a little punchy after court. The sky falls on you, you get punchy. If you know anything that would help, we could sure use it."

Harper spread his arms. "I don't have anything. I just wanted to warn you. Henry Firth is too happy. He may have something else."

"Or he could just be taking victory laps because of the surprise ID," Aaron said.

"It's a damaging revelation, but give me a break," Cora said. "Rick Reed may treat it like the case is over, but I can't see Becky folding her cards just like that. She hasn't even had her turn to bat yet."

"Good Lord," Aaron said. "You got Becky Baldwin playing poker and baseball at the same time. She's a pretty accomplished woman, but that seems a little much."

Sherry picked up Aaron's plate. "You want to eat or not?"

"I warned you about overpraising the ex," Cora said.

Harper put up his hands. "Okay, don't say I didn't warn you."

"We appreciate it," Cora said. "It's just a

little vague."

"I know. It's all I got."

"Well, what do you make of that?" Aaron said, after the chief had left.

"Beats me," Cora said. "If I didn't know better, I'd think Paula Martindale confessed."

"Could she do that?"

"In theory, not without her lawyer present. On the other hand, if she brought up copping a plea, Ratface could tell her self-righteously he couldn't listen to her and she should save it for court."

Aaron voiced an opinion that Jennifer echoed.

"Aaron!" Sherry said.

"Uh oh," Cora said. "Make room in the doghouse, Buddy."

"What do you *really* think it is?" Aaron said.

"I have no idea. At this point, nothing would surprise me."

"You've more or less written the client off, haven't you?" Sherry said.

"Why do you say that?"

"You're not investigating anymore. You're sitting in court looking to snipe. That's all it's become for you. Just an exercise in courtroom gymnastics."

"Whoa. What brought this on?"

"Not that I blame you. Not all cases are winners. Not all clients are innocent. It's just not like you to throw in the towel. And when I saw you did a crossword puzzle —"

"What!"

"And congratulations, by the way. I haven't solved it yet, but I am duly impressed."

"What the hell are you talking about?"

"Hell!"

"No fair," Cora said. "That wasn't at the end of the sentence."

"She's starting to learn the words," Aaron said.

"What's this about a crossword puzzle?"

"The one you constructed," Sherry said.

"Constructed?" Cora said. "I didn't just solve a puzzle, I made one up?"

"The one in 'Crossword Compiler.' I didn't solve it yet. Are you telling me it's meaningless, just a bunch of random letters?"

"I have no idea what you're talking about."

"In 'Crossword Compiler.' On your computer. You didn't start playing around with a puzzle grid?"

"Why in the world would I do that? Sherry, I don't think I could even *find* 'Crossword Compiler.' "

"There's an icon on the desktop."

"By 'desktop' you mean the main computer screen?"

"Well, if you didn't make up the puzzle, who did?"

Cora felt suddenly light-headed. "Oh, no! Where's the puzzle?"

"I printed it out. I was gonna solve it, but the macaroni was ready. Now, where did I put it?"

Sherry went down the hall, was back moments later with the puzzle. "Here you go. Does that ring a bell?"

"You're kidding, right? It's a crossword puzzle. Even I know that. It's not familiar; I can't imagine any reason why it should be. You gonna solve it?"

"I don't have to. The solution grid's in 'Crossword Compiler.' I'll just print it out."

"You can do that?"

"Of course."

Sherry was back in less than a minute, handed the solution grid to Cora.

Cora read the theme answer out loud. " 'Wanna know where he is? Wooing her with a kiss.' " Cora lowered the paper. "Oh, my God," she murmured. "It's all falling apart."

"So someone hacked our computer and uploaded a crossword puzzle," Sherry said. "I should have thought of it. It's happened before."

"Hacked," Cora said. "You mean with firewalls and all that other stuff I don't understand?"

"More likely someone snuck in when no one was here and plugged in a zip drive. It's not like you ever lock your door."

"Yeah," Cora said flatly. She looked utterly drained.

"What's the matter?"

"I'm Becky's investigator. I gotta bring this to her."

"Won't it help?"

"How could it help?"

"It corroborates her client's story."

"The client hasn't told her story."

"Well, this corroborates it."

"On the one hand," Cora said. "On the other hand, it nails down her motive."

"Didn't the desk clerk more or less do that?"

"The desk clerk doesn't tie it to my computer. Gotta call Becky."

Cora hurried from the room with a string of invectives more suitable to a biker bar.

Sherry leveled her finger at Jennifer. "You didn't hear that."

CHAPTER 28

Becky looked up from the puzzle. "What the hell!"

"Yeah," Cora said. "I thought she was making it up."

"So did I. Just because you're involved. I thought it gave her the idea. A ridiculous story that can't be proved but can't be disproved. And if we trot it out, people will think you dreamed it up. Because you're working for me. I had totally dismissed the idea of a crossword puzzle as not worth considering. And now you drop it in my lap."

"Hey, don't blame me," Cora said. "It's not like I made the damn thing up."

"Oh, no?" Becky said. "You didn't look at the case and say, 'Hey, this is hopeless, I gotta corroborate her story'?"

"And then left the puzzle on my own damn computer instead of printing it out and planting it where it would do some good?"

"Maybe you planted it, but no one found it."

"Are you kidding?"

"Or you planted it, someone found it, didn't know what it was, and threw it away. Or you planted it, someone found it, and decided to suppress it."

"Becky, this gets worse and worse. I didn't construct it, I didn't plant it, I had nothing to do with the goddamned thing. Someone loaded it into my computer. It's been done before, if you'll recall."

"Yeah, by a sadist who was targeting *you.* That's hardly the case here. Who would want to do that?"

"Aside from our client?"

"Our client?"

"She's a spiteful bitch. You should see her at the bridge table. She'd frame me for murder just for misdefending a Three No Trump contract."

"I don't know what that means. You're not being rational. Let's look at where we are."

"We're in the bar at the Country Kitchen," Cora said. "Because you ran out of scotch."

They were actually in a booth in the bar of the Country Kitchen and talking low, though no one appeared to be taking an interest in their conversation.

"I don't know what to do," Becky said. "If I tell my client, she's going to want to talk."

"Will you let her?"

"I don't know. I shouldn't have to make that decision until I put on my case. I don't think I can shut her up that long."

"I don't, either."

"If I don't tell her, she's liable to sue me for malpractice."

"How can she sue you for malpractice if she doesn't know we've got it?"

"Cora."

"I'm just sayin'."

Becky sighed. "The puzzle provides the missing motive. It's a prosecutor's dream."

"Only if he can prove she saw it."

"She's going to admit she saw it. She's going to shout it from the housetops."

"So what if she saw it? It's no motive unless she solved it."

"She *did* solve it."

"She doesn't have to say so."

"Oh, great," Becky said. "Now you got me suborning perjury."

"It's not necessarily perjury. Our client says a lot of things. Some of them turn out to be true."

"Except following her husband to the hotel."

"She didn't say she didn't. She just didn't mention it."

"A sin of omission," Becky said.

"Didn't she say she had a perfect marriage, her husband would never do that?"

"Yeah, but wives say that."

"I sure didn't. Just ask Melvin."

Becky shook her head. "This is very bad. I have attorney-client privilege. You don't. You are withholding evidence."

"Evidence of what? It's a crossword puzzle. I don't know where it came from. I don't know it has anything to do with anything."

"My client told you it did."

"Oh, now it's 'my' client. She's your client, and I'm withholding evidence. Correct me if I'm wrong, but your client hasn't identified this puzzle as the one she claims she saw, and it would be irresponsible on my part to go running to the police and level an accusation of that type based on such flimsy evidence."

"Accusation?"

"I may have exaggerated a little. I'm not sure what degree of slander we're talking about here."

Becky took a sip of her scotch, considered. "You make a strong case."

Cora shrugged. "That's because I'm not a lawyer."

CHAPTER 29

Sherry squeezed in next to Cora in the front row.

"Back again?" Cora said.

"After last night I wouldn't miss it."

"I'm hoping there's nothing to miss."

"What are the odds of that?"

"Not good."

"Does your client know about the you-know-what?"

"Bite your tongue."

Court was called to order, and Bob Krantz resumed the stand.

"Now, then," Judge Hobbs said. "When we adjourned the prosecution was conducting its direct examination of Mr. Krantz. Mr. Firth, do you have any further questions for the witness?"

"No, Your Honor. That's all."

Becky got to her feet. "Mr. Krantz, you testified that you saw my client at the hotel?"

"That's right."

"On how many occasions?"

"Just the one."

"And when would that be?"

"On the sixth of June."

"And how do you fix the date?"

"It's one of the days her husband stayed there."

"Did she come with him?"

"No."

"Did she ask for him at the desk?"

"No, she did not."

"So you didn't know it at the time."

Bob Krantz frowned. "I beg your pardon?"

"There was nothing to connect my client to her husband at the time. So when you say she was there the same day he was there, you're doing it in retrospect. You're saying, 'He was there on the sixth, so I must have seen her on the sixth.' Isn't that right?"

"No, it is not."

"Correct me where I'm wrong."

"When I saw her I realized that was the woman I saw on the sixth. Her husband was also there on the sixth. I can't help the fact she was there the same day as her husband, it just so happens she was. You may not like it, but it's a fact."

"What thing, besides the presence of her husband, allows you to pinpoint the fact she was there on the sixth?"

190

"Nothing in particular. I just remember that she was."

"How?"

"I have a good memory."

"Having a good memory is one thing, Mr. Krantz, but you can't remember something that you've never known. I put it to you that you never knew my client was there on the sixth, so you can't remember it."

"Well, it's probably not the first time you've been mistaken."

That sally was greeted by a burst of laughter from the courtroom.

Becky smiled at the witness. "Mr. Krantz, I don't mean to badger you, I'm just trying to understand your thought process. It's not often we get a witness as observant as you are, with a memory as good as yours. When you saw my client, was there anything in particular that drew your attention to her?"

"She was hesitant about being there. She paused in the doorway and waited until the elevator door had closed. Then she came in, went to the elevator bank, and looked up at the readout that indicates which floor it's on. She didn't wait for it, however. When the elevator started down, she turned around and went outside."

"Did she come back after that?"

"No, she did not."

"When you saw her do this, was that right after her husband had come in and gotten in the elevator?"

"I really couldn't say. As you pointed out, I had not yet connected the two things in my mind. I know the time he came in because it's in the registration. She didn't register, so I'm guessing. I would guess it was around the time, but I'm not sure."

"Thank you, Mr. Krantz. No further questions."

"Any redirect?" Judge Hobbs said.

"I have one or two more questions," Henry Firth said. "Mr. Krantz, you say you can't tell whether you saw the defendant in the lobby of the hotel at the same time her husband checked in?"

"Yes, I can."

"You can? And was it the same time her husband checked in?"

"No, it was not. When the defendant came in the front door, there was no one at the desk. I had a completely unobstructed view of the front door. If someone had been checking in, he'd have been in my line of sight."

"Is it possible she came in immediately after her husband checked in?"

"It's entirely possible, but I didn't see it happen, so I can't testify to it."

"And on the other day that her husband checked in, you did not notice her on that day?"

"No, I did not."

"As far as you know, she was not there?"

"I didn't say that. All I can say is I didn't see her. If she was there, I missed her."

"But you don't know if she was there?"

"No, I do not."

"Let me ask you this. On the day her husband was there that you *didn't* see her there, did you see anyone else?"

"Lots of people. It's a hotel. People check in, people check out."

"I mean anyone associated with this case."

"Oh. As a matter of fact, I did."

"Are you saying that on the other day her husband checked in, you saw someone in this courtroom other than the defendant in that hotel?"

"That's right."

"And who would that be?"

"The woman in the front row right behind the lady lawyer asking all the questions."

Bob Krantz pointed his finger straight at Cora Felton.

CHAPTER 30

"What a mess," Becky said.

"You're telling *me,*" Cora said. "It's enough to make me start smoking."

"It's enough to make me start smoking *crack.* What the hell were you thinking?"

Cora gave Becky a look. "Are you kidding me?"

"No, I know what you were thinking. What made you think you could get away with it?"

"Becky. You're very young. Well, maybe not as young as you look. But you're adorably naive. Getting away with it is not a high priority in my lifestyle. Enjoying the moment has a lot more appeal."

"You were having an affair with Roger Martindale."

"Does that surprise you?"

"Nothing you do surprises me. Isn't he a little young for you?"

Cora grimaced. "Please. It's bad enough

to be accused of murder. Let's not get personal."

Following the Bob Krantz revelation, Cora had been taken into custody. While a specific charge was not named, the smart money was on murder. The only real obstacle to a speedy prosecution was the fact that Henry Firth already had one suspect on trial. But there was no doubt he would be happy to swap defendants. Convicting Paula Martindale would be a feather in his cap. Convicting the Puzzle Lady would be a career maker.

"It's going to get personal, Cora. It's going to get very personal. Every indiscretion you ever committed is going to get aired in open court."

"Are you going to let that happen?"

"Not without a fight. But the questions I can block are going to hurt you worse than the ones you have to answer. People are going to think, *What she's hiding must be terrific.*"

"It was."

"Cora."

"I can't help it. I got my heart broken for the thousandth time. Crowley has a girlfriend. And I like her, and I don't want to bust them up. And that's not a situation I'm used to dealing with. Is it any surprise I found somebody else?"

"But Roger Martindale?"

"What's wrong with Roger Martindale? Aside from being dead, I mean."

"You play bridge with his wife."

"She's a spiteful bitch. I don't feel bad about cheating on Paula Martindale. Cheating on Paula Martindale is an added perk."

"Well, she happens to be my client, which is a bit of a problem."

"Why?"

"You'll have to get a lawyer."

"What?"

"I can't represent you both. It's a conflict of interest. I'm not like a prosecutor. I'm not allowed to dump one defendant just because a better one comes along."

"You've got to be kidding."

"I'm not. Oh, I can do it. I'm a lawyer, I more or less do anything I want."

"May I quote you on that?"

"But I'd like to do it in ways that don't involve the bar association."

"If that's the case, why are you talking to me now?"

"Well, someone has to. But you really have to hire your own attorney."

"So get me out of here."

Becky made a face. "Well, that's a problem. If I push 'em too hard, they'll charge you. If they charge you, I'll be in a position where I can't represent you because it will be a conflict of interest. So I won't be able to get you out because I won't be able to represent you."

"Are you messing with me?"

"Just a little. If my client asks me not to represent you —"

"Why would she do that?"

"You were sleeping with her husband."

"Oh, you think she might take offense?"

"Cora."

"All right, all right, she probably doesn't like me. I don't like her, either. Why is this even an issue? As soon as Ratface gets done posturing about his wonderful courtroom revelation, it's going to dawn on him that in the typical marital triangle it's the aggrieved wife who gets pissed off enough to hack up her husband, not the woman who happens to like him."

"What if he was dumping her and going back to his wife?"

"What, play the woman-scorned card? Not nearly as good. And speaking of likely suspects, who would you pick, the woman covered in blood clutching a butcher knife, or the woman who arrived with the chief of police and caught her at the crime scene with the murder weapon?"

"Ordinarily, that would be true."

"Ordinarily? What, this is a special case? It's the Puzzle Lady, let's dork her?"

"No, it's the Puzzle Lady, and there's a puzzle involved."

"Oh, for Christ's sakes."

"See the problem?"

"Are you going to tell them about the crossword puzzle?"

"No, but my client will."

"She doesn't know about it."

Becky said nothing.

Cora's eyes widened. "You're going to tell her?"

"She's my client."

"*I'm* your client. The crossword puzzle has nothing to do with the current situation. Assuming it ever existed, she took it to the mall and burned it."

"It's on your computer."

"*A* crossword is on my computer. You don't know that it's the one she was talking about. She couldn't remember what it said. There's so many other things on the table right now, why would you want to clutter up the scene with that?"

Becky took a breath. "I'll do what I can."

"Can you get me out of here?"

"I'll try."

Becky left the interrogation room, hunted

up Henry Firth. "She's not talking. Charge her or release her."

CHAPTER 31

Rick Reed was waiting to pounce. "Here's Cora Felton now. Ms. Felton, is it true you were having an affair with the murdered man?"

"Hi, Rick. Nice day. Good to see you."

"Can you answer the question?"

"What question?"

"Were you having an affair with the murdered man?"

"The dead man?"

"Yes."

"It's very hard to have an affair with a dead man."

"Before he was killed."

"Before he was killed?"

"Yes."

"Before he was killed, he wasn't a dead man." Cora smiled, patted him on the cheek. "You really seem confused about this, Rick. Figure it out and we'll talk."

"From your evasive answers I'm inclined

to think you were."

"Oh, I doubt that."

"You doubt that you were having an affair with the victim?"

"No, I doubt that you're inclined to think. I've never found you inclined to think, Rick. In fact, thinking is the last thing I ever would have suspected you of."

"And there you have it," Rick said. "The Puzzle Lady, dodging questions like a common criminal. If I hadn't seen it with my own eyes, I wouldn't have believed it."

There was a knock on Cora's bedroom door. Aaron Grant came in. She muted the TV. "What's up?"

"Anything I should know?" Aaron said.

Cora made a face. "Not you, too."

"No, not me, too," Aaron said. "I'm not one of those buzzards circling to pick at the corpse. I just wondered if there was anything I could do to help."

"Confess to killing Roger Martindale."

"That wasn't what I had in mind."

"That wasn't what I had in mind, either. But somehow, that's what people expect of me. Pretty stupid when you think about it. Why would I want to kill Roger Martindale?"

"To protect your good name."

"What good name? The one my umpteenth husband Melvin is always dragging in the dirt? It's not like a hint of scandal could hurt me."

"Yes and no."

"You're the second person who's done that to me lately. The first one, I almost took his head off. You care to explain, or are you auditioning to make the front page of the *New York Post*?"

"A scandal doesn't bother you. But it might bother Granville Grains."

"Oh, I don't think so. I've been in the tabloids before."

"Not for killing an adulterous lover."

"Oh, God, you're right." Cora frowned. Considered. "Except."

"Except what?"

"You're talking about a motive. Why I killed Roger. Saying 'to cover up the fact I killed Roger' isn't really fair."

"That's not what I meant."

"I know it isn't. It's only what you said. Becky Baldwin would love to have a go at you in court. Speaking of adulterous relationships."

Aaron's mouth fell open. "I am not having an affair with Becky Baldwin."

"Neither was Barney Nathan, but everyone thought he was. I certainly hope you don't fall into the same trap."

"Are you threatening me with Becky Baldwin?"

"Absolutely not, and you can quote me on that: 'Cora Felton denies saying anything about an affair between Aaron Grant and Becky Baldwin.' "

Aaron put up his hands. "Hey, I wasn't attacking you. I was only telling you how the prosecution's going to see it."

"And I was telling you why it's a stupid idea. As stupid as pairing you with Becky Baldwin. Which I have no intention of doing, by the way. But I see your point. Granville Grains would not be happy to see me in an affair with a married man. But the idea that a married man was threatening to expose his own affair with me just for the purpose of smearing my name, when it would get him in trouble as well, is really a stretch. And when you throw in the idea that I killed him to prevent that from happening, well, Becky Baldwin could defend that murder charge in her sleep." Cora shrugged. "If it weren't for the conflict of interest."

"She can't represent you?"

"Not while she's representing Paula Martindale."

"Any way you could get her fired?"

"Aaron!"

"Hey, I'm on your side. Anything I could write that Paula Martindale might find objectionable?"

"You *are* just looking for a story."

"I'm *always* looking for a story. I'm not looking for a story that trashes you. Which probably puts me in a distinct minority at the moment."

The phone on Cora's bedside table rang. She scooped it up.

It was Becky. "Meet me at the Country Kitchen. Fast as you can get there."

"Why?"

"Sky is falling."

CHAPTER 32

Cora raced down to the Country Kitchen, hurried into the bar. Becky wasn't there. Cora was torn between leaving and hurling a bar stool through the mirror.

Before she could decide, Becky came in.

"You're here," Becky said. "Good. Let's go."

"Go? I just got here."

"You're just leaving."

"What's up?"

"Tell you in the car."

Becky turned on her heel and was gone before Cora could strangle her. Cora stomped out the door, steam coming from her ears. Becky was halfway across the parking lot. Cora headed for her car.

"Leave it. Ride with me," Becky said.

Cora rolled her eyes and followed Becky to her car. She got in and slammed the door with more than her usual force.

"Easy," Becky said. "Small car, could fall apart."

"What the hell is going on?" Cora demanded.

"Let me get out of here."

Becky switched on the lights, backed up, pulled out of the parking lot.

"Can we talk *now*?" Cora said.

"She spilled her guts."

"What?"

"My client. My all-time-favorite client, Paula Martindale. She went behind my back to the police."

"She can't do that."

"Well, she did. I'm sure Henry Firth will say he advised her she had to have her attorney present. And I'm sure she will say she told him she didn't care. And I'm sure he got that portion of her statement taken down so he can prove she said it."

"Where are we going?"

"We're going for a ride, and don't you forget it. If anyone asks, we're trying to avoid Rick Reed and the local media. We're certainly not avoiding the police, and we had no idea they were looking for us."

"Are they looking for us?"

"I can't imagine why they wouldn't be."

"Why?"

"I told you. Paula Martindale made a

statement."

"What did she say?"

"Everything. She told them everything she knows. Including the crossword puzzle."

"But she doesn't know we have it."

"No. If she did, you'd probably be in jail."

"You're kidding."

"It was on your computer. You do the math."

Cora did the math. Her conclusion was unprintable in most major publications.

"Exactly," Becky said. "Clearly, you've been framed. The question is by whom."

"That's grammatically correct."

"What's wrong with it?"

"I *know* by whom. Your lying, no-good client did it. She figured I was having an affair with her husband, so she killed him and framed me for it."

"By framing herself?"

"It is a novel twist. But it certainly makes the case against me more believable."

"How's that?"

"By making it unbelievable she would have done it."

"That's the most convoluted double-think I've ever heard."

"Exactly."

"Not hers. Yours. That's going to be your defense? That Paula Martindale framed you by framing herself so it wouldn't look like she framed you?"

"Well, when you put it that way, it sounds kind of stupid."

"Well, would you mind putting it so it doesn't sound stupid? I've been mixed up with Paula Martindale too damn long, and I'm sick to death of stupid."

"Well, if she didn't frame me, someone else did. Someone sent her a puzzle, someone put it on my computer."

"Why?"

"Why what?"

"Why would they do that? If they actually were framing Paula Martindale, why would they involve you?"

"Oh."

"Hadn't thought of it?"

"I haven't thought of much else. It just keeps going around in my head. It's not surprising, the way things are working out. They framed Paula Martindale because they wanted to frame Paula Martindale, not because they wanted to frame me. I don't know why they wanted to frame Paula Martindale, but they did. You have to go back to why they killed Roger Martindale. They either killed Roger Martindale because they *wanted* to kill Roger Martindale, or because they wanted to *frame* Paula Martindale.

Which sounds like the same thing but isn't. It depends what the ultimate goal was, eliminating him or blaming her.

"In either event, the framing of Paula Martindale was at least partly to shift the blame, so the real killer wouldn't be suspected. Framing me is secondary. It's an afterthought. It serves two purposes. If the case against Paula Martindale falls apart, I'm the backup. The blame shifts to me. I, rather than the actual killer, am next in line.

"That's one reason. The other reason is he wanted to lure Paula Martindale out of the house so he could kill her husband. He did it with the crossword puzzle, which was diabolically clever. Because he had her burn it. So if she told her story, it couldn't be proven. But if her story was believed, the crossword puzzle would eventually be traced back to the one on my computer."

"How did he even know she could solve a crossword puzzle?" Becky said.

"He didn't, but it didn't matter. That was the clever part. He wrote a message on the top, telling her to go to the mall and burn the puzzle. As long as she did that, everything was fine. It happened she *did* solve the puzzle, which was good, because it gave her more reason to go to the mall, but the killer didn't really care as long as it got her out of the house.

"The killer is watching from the road, with Roger Martindale in the trunk of his car. The minute the killer sees her take off for the mall, he lugs the body inside. He has no trouble getting in, because he has Roger's keys. He flops him on the living room rug, gets a butcher knife from the kitchen, and stabs him."

Cora broke off. "Hey. Where the hell are we going?"

"Hang on," Becky said. "We're almost there."

"Almost where?" Cora said. "We're half-way to Danbury."

"Yeah, that's probably far enough," Becky said. She pulled off the road into a motel parking lot.

"You turning around?" Cora said.

"Yeah," Becky said. "Just hang on a moment, will you?"

Becky hopped out of the car, went in the office. She was back minutes later. She drove up in front of unit six, slapped a key in Cora's hand. "Here you go. You're registered as Susie Benson. Go in, lie down, take it easy, watch some TV. You got all the cable channels, including free HBO. You can call out for pizza, but don't use your credit card, pay cash. And don't call Sherry and Aaron and tell 'em where you are."

"Come on," Cora said. "What's the big idea?"

"You're upset over being publicly accused of having an affair with a married man. You don't want to be hounded by the tabloids."

"No, not the reason I *claim* I'm doing this. The *real* reason I'm doing this."

"I'm not your lawyer. I don't want the cops to pick you up if I can't protect you."

"I have to hang out here until you solve the case?"

"No, just until things quiet down."

"How long will that be?"

"Probably never."

"Becky."

"For the time being, I need you out of circulation. It can't be helped, but it shouldn't be long."

"Can we get away with it?"

"I think so. We've got one thing going for us."

"What's that?"

"I'm not your lawyer."

CHAPTER 33

"I can't help you."

Chief Harper frowned. "What do you mean, you can't help me? I'm the chief of police."

Becky smiled. "Yes, you are. And I think you're doing a great job."

"Don't mess with me, Becky. I'm not in a good mood. I want Cora Felton."

"You had her. You released her."

"That was before your client talked."

"Funny you should mention it, Chief. Was that violation of my client's rights all Rat-face's doing, or did you have a hand in it?"

"No one violated anyone's rights. Your client was advised she didn't have to talk. If she chose to ignore that advice, it's not our fault."

"So you are taking some of the blame."

"No one's taking any blame. Everything was strictly by the book."

"May I quote you on that, Chief? When I

get you on the stand, I mean?"

"Your client made a statement of her own free will. She threw Cora Felton under the bus. It seems there's a relevant crossword puzzle she neglected to mention. You neglected to mention it, too, but I'm sure you'll claim attorney-client privilege. Which may or may not hold up in court, because Cora was apparently a third party to the conversation. At least that's Henry Firth's opinion, and in matters of procedure he's apt to be right."

"Can you give me an example of that, Chief? I find myself hard-pressed to think of one."

Harper grimaced, put up his hand. "Please, I'm not in the mood. Whether you can be compelled to tell about the crossword puzzle is debatable. Whether Cora can is not. She's a private citizen, she doesn't have attorney-client privilege. If she withholds material evidence in a murder investigation, she can go to jail."

"I'll be sure to tell her, Chief. Though it's a relatively elementary rule of law, so I imagine she already knows."

"I'm not asking you to take her a message. I'm asking you to surrender her to the police."

"Oh, dear."

"Oh, dear?"

"Sorry, Chief, I can't do that."

"You can and you will. Or Henry Firth will get a court order. Then if you don't you'll be in contempt of court."

"I doubt that very much."

Harper picked up the phone, punched in a number. "She's here . . . No, her lawyer . . . Says she won't . . . Okay." He hung up the phone. "He'll be right over."

"Who?"

"Henry Firth."

"The prosecutor himself? Coming to see little old me? I feel flattered."

"You won't when he gets here."

"We'll see."

Henry Firth was there in five minutes. Becky had the feeling he'd been waiting for the call. He was clearly agitated but made every effort to start off calmly.

"Now then, young lady, what seems to be the trouble?"

"No trouble at all. Thanks to Judge Hobbs granting a continuance, I was catching up on my paperwork when Chief Harper asked me to stop by."

"He mention that I wanted to talk to Cora Felton?"

"I believe the subject came up."

"Then why isn't she here?"

"You'll have to ask her."

"I can't ask her. She isn't here."

"Hmm. That would seem to present a problem."

"It presents a little more than that. Cora Felton is, at the very least, a material witness in a murder investigation. I've got a court order requiring you to produce her. Do you intend to do so?"

"Oh, I think not," Becky said.

"Then you're in for a rude shock, little lady. Judge Hobbs has a low tolerance for those who play fast and loose with the law."

"And rightfully so," Becky said. "It's disgraceful what some people try to get away with."

"Yes, yes, very clever," Henry said. "But you know what you sound like? You sound like someone whistling in the dark. Putting up a good front. It's what people do when they're losing."

"You must have had a lot of practice," Becky said.

"You have until four o'clock this afternoon to produce Cora Felton in court."

"Court's not in session this afternoon."

"Yes, it is. After he signed the warrant, Judge Hobbs did me the courtesy of going to his courtroom. I don't want to tell you your business, but if I were you I'd produce

Cora Felton as soon as possible, because the longer you make Judge Hobbs sit there, the less likely he's going to be receptive to your argument."

"May I quote you on that, Henry? 'Judge Hobbs is likely to let personal grudges affect his decisions.' "

"That's not what I said and you know it. Are you going to produce Cora Felton?"

Becky smiled. "According to you, I don't have to do it till four o'clock."

"Are you going to let Judge Hobbs sit there all day?"

"Well, Henry, you make a good point. What do you say we mosey over to the courthouse?"

Henry Firth, who had expected more of an argument, said, "Good idea."

Chief Harper left Dan Finley in charge of the station and tagged along.

Judge Hobbs was eating a sandwich and reading the newspaper. He frowned when they came in. "Ms. Baldwin. Where is your client?"

"Still in jail, I'm afraid. Were you thinking of granting bail?"

"Not her. Cora Felton."

"Oh. I'm sorry, Your Honor, Cora Felton's not my client."

"Yes, she is," Henry Firth said. "You've

been acting on her behalf. That's the reason she's not here now. You told me charge her or release her."

"Sure, I did. But I wasn't acting as her attorney. I was acting as a friend."

"If you're not Cora Felton's attorney, who is?"

"I don't know. I'm not sure she has one."

"If she doesn't have one, it's because you are."

"I don't follow the reasoning. If she doesn't have a violin teacher, does that mean I must be it?"

"Your Honor," Henry Firth said. "Look at the slimy way she's attempting to squirm her way out of it. If you ask me, it's sharp practice."

"Not at all, Your Honor. I'm not Cora Felton's lawyer because I can't be Cora Felton's lawyer. I'm Paula Martindale's lawyer. I can't represent Cora Felton, particularly if there is any chance she could be charged with Roger Martindale's murder. It's a flagrant conflict of interest."

Judge Hobbs smiled. "I'm afraid she's got you there, Henry. If Cora Felton's in any way a suspect, clearly, Becky can't represent her while Paula Martindale's on trial for the crime."

"Unless you want to dismiss the charges,

Henry," Becky said sweetly.

Judge Hobbs cut short the prosecutor's indignant denial. "Yes, yes," he said, a twinkle in his eye. "The court notes your disinclination to dismiss."

"Well," Becky said. "I'm glad that's cleared up. If you don't mind, I do have some trial prep."

"I *do* mind," Henry Firth said. "I want to know where Cora Felton is."

"I understand your feelings."

"It's more than just my feelings. Cora Felton is a material witness in a murder investigation. If you refuse to divulge her whereabouts, that's obstruction of justice."

"Oh, my," Becky said. "And that would be against the law?"

"You know damn well it's against the law."

"I could go to jail for it?"

"You certainly could."

"That simplifies the situation. In that case, I would have to refuse to answer on the grounds that an answer might tend to incriminate me."

"Then you know where Cora Felton is?"

"I'm not saying that. I'm just saying I won't answer your questions. It must be frustrating for you. Try not to take it personally."

"What about the crossword puzzle?"

"What crossword puzzle?"

"The one your client had."

"I'm glad you brought that up," Becky said. "Are you referring to a crossword puzzle my client told you about when you questioned her outside of my presence?"

"Your client made a statement of her own volition."

"When you questioned her outside of my presence?"

"I didn't question her. She chose to make a statement."

"Did you have that statement taken down?"

"What's that got to do with it?"

"I'd love to see it," Becky said. "Particularly since you now claim you asked no questions during that statement."

"That's not what I said."

"I asked you if you questioned her, you said no, she made a statement. Which is it? Did you question her or not?"

"Your Honor, I don't have to submit to a cross-examination."

"You will when you try to admit my client's 'voluntary' statement in court."

"It won't do you any good. Your client specifically declined to have an attorney present."

"That's going to be your defense?"

"Defense? I'm not the defendant here, no matter how much you try to cloud the issues."

"I'm trying to clarify the issues. You keep making statements that are inherently false. Am I supposed to take them as fact just because you're the county prosecutor?"

"Are we done here?" Judge Hobbs asked.

"Not by a long shot," Henry Firth said. "I want to know about the crossword puzzle. She keeps changing the subject."

"Another misstatement of fact," Becky pointed out.

"Oh, really?" Henry Firth said. "Your client got a crossword puzzle telling her to go to the mall. She claims she went to the mall, burned the crossword puzzle, and waited as instructed. When no one showed up, she went home and found her husband murdered."

"Thank you for telling me what my client said."

"You know what your client said. And you know what your client thought when she heard Cora Felton had been in that hotel with her husband. She thought, who else would have lured her away from the house with a crossword puzzle?"

Becky's smile was enormous. "She thought *Cora Felton* sent her a crossword

220

puzzle to frame her for the murder of her husband?"

"You know that's what she thought."

"Of course," Becky said sarcastically. "The Puzzle Lady frames her rival for murder with a crossword puzzle. Who would ever suspect? It would be the perfect crime."

Henry Firth frowned. "Let's not quibble. Do you have that crossword puzzle?"

"That was burned at the mall?"

"Do you have a copy of that puzzle?"

"A hypothetical copy of a hypothetical puzzle my client mentioned when you illegally questioned her outside of my presence?"

"There was nothing illegal about it."

"Let's not go around again," Judge Hobbs said. "Ms. Baldwin. Do I understand that you have no intention of revealing Cora Felton's whereabouts or discussing any evidence your client may have mentioned to the prosecuting attorney?'

"That's right, Your Honor."

"Good. I'm going home."

CHAPTER 34

There was a knock on the door. Cora got up, leaned close, said, "Who is it?"

"Open up. It's me."

Cora eased the motel door open. Crowley and Stephanie came in.

"Were you followed?" Cora said.

"No."

"Are you sure?"

"I'm a policeman."

"Sorry. I'm just nervous."

Stephanie surveyed the sparse motel room furnishings. "Hey, nice place you got here."

"I didn't choose it for the decor."

"I imagine not. Any reason you couldn't come see us in New York? Not that I mind driving out here or anything."

"It would have meant crossing state lines. Flight is an indication of guilt."

"You really think they'll charge you?" Crowley said.

"The only thing stopping them is they

can't find me," Cora said. "You can probably score some brownie points by turning me in."

"Hey, it's not like I had a choice. I had to give up the desk clerk. How was I supposed to know he was going to finger you? I can't be expected to keep track of all your romantic entanglements."

"Oh, low blow," Stephanie said. "You sanctimonious one-woman man."

"You're enjoying this, aren't you?" Cora said.

"No. You're a friend and you're in trouble. But it is kind of amusing. I mean, it's not like anyone seriously thinks you killed the guy. You never killed any of your husbands."

"Well, I was never prosecuted for it," Cora said.

Crowley gave her a look.

"Hey, when you've had as many husbands as I have, some of them are going to die. It's not my fault, it's just statistics."

"Are you sure they're going to arrest you?" Stephanie said.

"I can't imagine why they wouldn't. Well, actually, I can. They have Paula Martindale on trial. It would be embarrassing to arrest me for the same crime. But they can arrest me for obstruction of justice."

"And now that we know it, they can arrest

us," Stephanie said. "Thanks a lot."

Cora grinned. "I hadn't thought of that. But now that you mention it . . ."

Crowley flopped down on the edge of the bed. "I don't get it."

"Get what?"

"This isn't like you. Running and hiding. I'd expect you to stride in there and take them all on."

"Oh, give her a break," Stephanie said. "She just had her affair aired in court. Of course she needs a little time to regroup."

"That's not it," Cora said. "You think I've never done the walk of shame before? I'd be perfectly happy to face the music. But Becky hasn't had a case in months. Then she gets the most depressing client imaginable. The type you can't help secretly hoping gets convicted. And she suddenly gets a chance to play Perry Mason. Spiriting away a witness. Taking on the court and the prosecutor. Finding legal ways not to surrender me. I can't bear to spoil her fun."

"That's why you're doing this?" Crowley said.

"Plus, I can use the time to try to figure out what the hell is going on. Before someone asks me to explain it and I haven't got a clue."

"This gets worse and worse," Stephanie

224

said. "We're not just obstructing justice. We're aiding and abetting a fugitive."

"Yeah." Cora cocked her head. "Kind of fun, isn't it?"

"So what do you expect us to do?" Crowley said.

"Do?"

"What was so all-fired important you called us up here? I mean, it's a hell of a situation, but I'm a New York City cop. What do you expect me to do about it?"

"I don't expect you to do anything," Cora said.

"Then why did you call?"

"I was lonely."

"Cora."

"I'm serious. Think about it. I'm stuck here without a car. I'm not allowed to call Sherry or Aaron because people will be asking them where I am. All I've had to eat for two days is pizza. I need to talk to a human being. I need to eat some decent food. Hell, maybe we could go to a movie."

"You're nutty as ever," Crowley said.

"Thank you."

There was a knock on the door. They looked at each other. Stephanie got up and opened it.

Becky came in. "What are you guys doing here?"

"Cora invited us for dinner and a movie," Stephanie said. "Wanna come?"

"No. I wanna talk to my client."

"I'm not your client," Cora said.

"You are now," Becky said grimly.

CHAPTER 35

"Paula Martindale fired me."

"Why?"

"She's a bitch."

"No kidding. Care to elaborate?"

"Cops got a warrant to search your house, found the puzzle on your computer. Paula flipped out, accused you of murdering her husband. Accused me of covering it up and helping you frame her for the crime."

"There's an idea."

"Cora."

"I'm just sayin'. You're no longer her attorney."

Becky pulled out around a slow-moving truck. An oncoming car hit the horn and slammed on the brakes as she pulled back in.

"What's the hurry?" Cora said.

"I want to surrender you before the police pick you up. I got enough problems without Henry Firth arguing you took to flight."

"I didn't take to flight. You flew me. I'd have been happy hanging out at home."

"Then they'd have picked you up when I wasn't your attorney. What would you have done then?"

"Told them to go to hell."

"Right. Which might not have been good for my client. Who at the time wasn't you."

"Yeah, but —"

"Cora. Let's not bicker. What's done is done. You're my client now, and it doesn't look good. You were having an affair with the murdered man."

"Allegedly."

"You *weren't* having an affair with the murdered man?"

"Well, there's no reason to concede the point."

"I'm your lawyer. I'll make the legal arguments. Right now I'd like to know what's true."

"You know what's true. The cops found the puzzle on my computer. I didn't put it there, I don't know how it got there. It's a clumsy-as-hell frame, and I can't see it holding up in court. Unless the cops have something else."

"They have you in the hotel with Roger Martindale."

"No, they don't. A substitute desk clerk

saw me there once. And not with Roger Martindale. Just in the hotel. And the regular desk clerk never saw me at all."

"Are you sure of that?"

"Absolutely. The guy's star-struck. When Crowley and I questioned him he recognized me as the Puzzle Lady and went nuts. If he'd have seen me before he'd have known it."

"You're saying you weren't there?"

"I'm not saying anything. But I am a recognizable celebrity. If I were sneaking off to a hotel to meet a married man, don't you think I'd make damn sure not to be seen?"

"The substitute clerk saw you."

"He thinks he did. He could be wrong."

"Shall I plan my courtroom strategy on that assumption?"

"Oh, come on. They're really going to put me on trial?"

"They released Paula Martindale. You think they did that on a whim?"

Becky was peeking out from behind a slow-moving Subaru as she negotiated an S-turn.

"I see your strategy," Cora said. "If you kill us both, we don't have to worry about it."

"What *should* I be worried about?" Becky said.

"What do you mean?"

"Besides the hotel? You have any other little surprises?"

"What difference does it make?"

"Well, it would be nice to know the death penalty's off the table."

"I thought Connecticut repealed the death penalty."

"For you they'd bring it back."

"There's no surprises, Becky. That's all they've got. I can't believe they're seriously considering trying me."

"I can't, either. But they wouldn't have let Paula Martindale go if they didn't think they had a better case against you."

"Chief Harper's not talking?"

"He's not talking to *me*. He might talk to *you*."

"He better."

"I'll send him by the lockup."

"That's not funny."

"It's no joke. There's a bench warrant out for your arrest."

"What?"

"Oh, did I miss that tidbit? That's why I'm so eager to get you back. Or at least be heading toward Bakerhaven instead of away from it when we get picked up."

Cora glanced around. "Now you got *me* worried. You sure you weren't followed?"

"Cops and robbers is your game. I'm not sure of anything."

Cora shook her head. "I can't believe they let her go. I'm just not a good-enough suspect. Not on the evidence. I mean, what have they got?"

CHAPTER 36

Chief Harper closed the door of the cell. "Sorry about this."

"You're sorry," Cora said.

"I have my orders."

"Please. Don't get me started on I-was-only-following-orders."

"All right. And I won't give you the it's-my-job bit, either. They both happen to be true."

"What's he got on me, Chief?"

Harper's eyes shifted.

"Uh oh. You got orders about that, too?"

"Henry Firth read me the riot act. He doesn't like the way this case has developed. He thinks the police work has been substandard. He's making a big deal about whether I'm a public official or whether I'm working with you."

"Oh, for God's sakes."

"I tell you, he's not happy, Cora. You know how bad it looks, changing defendants in mid-prosecution."

"Oh, there's a concept. Ratface concerned about his looks."

"I'm glad you can still joke about it."

"I can't still joke about it. I would like to talk to you about it. Like two friends. Like two colleagues. Like two people who have worked together. But — oh, no — you're playing this arms-length, Henry-Firth-wouldn't-want-me-to, and I'm supposed to understand. I'm in jail charged with murder, and I'm supposed to understand."

"You had the crossword puzzle on your machine."

"Someone planted something in my office. Not a novel concept in the annals of criminal behavior."

"There's other evidence."

"What other evidence?"

"It will all come out in the trial."

"I don't want to go to trial."

"That's not my decision."

"You're saying you can't help me."

"Did you kill him?"

"Of course I didn't kill him."

"Then you got nothing to worry about."

"Now I'm *really* worried."

CHAPTER 37

Rick Reed couldn't have been happier. "Martindale murder trial, take two!" he proclaimed in a Channel 8 on-camera remote in front of the police station. "That's right, ladies and gentlemen, in an unprecedented move, County Prosecutor Henry Firth dismissed the charges against Paula Martindale in mid-trial and is proceeding instead against Bakerhaven's own beloved Puzzle Lady, Cora Felton."

The TV cut to a shot of the courthouse steps.

"I caught up with Henry Firth earlier this afternoon."

Rick Reed thrust a microphone in the prosecutor's face.

"Mr. Firth, I understand you intend to try Cora Felton for the crime. Do you have the right woman this time?"

Henry Firth's response was largely bleeped out.

"There you have it," Rick Reed said. "Bakerhaven's own Puzzle Lady Cora Felton is now charged with the crime. And judging from his first response, the prosecutor isn't happy about it. One can only wonder, who will he charge tomorrow?"

"Good point," Cora said.

Aaron Grant dropped his taco. He grabbed the zapper, froze the TV. "Oh, my God. Mark it on the calendar. Cora Felton actually believes Rick Reed has a good point."

Jennifer, who was having too much fun dropping tacos of her own, missed the opportunity to yell, "Point!"

Buddy, on the other hand, didn't miss the opportunity to wolf up the scattered food.

Sherry took a taco shell off the tray, filled it with lettuce, tomato, meat, cheese, and guacamole. "Of course he has a good point. But don't give him any credit. Any moron outside of the county prosecutor knows that charging you is stupid."

"Let's just hope twelve jurors agree."

"They're not going to find twelve jurors in Bakerhaven willing to consider you guilty."

"They're not supposed to," Cora said. "They're supposed to consider me innocent."

"*Not* because they're prejudiced in your favor."

"That's not my problem. That's Henry Firth's problem. I hope it's not his *only* problem."

"You can't find out what they've got against you?" Sherry asked.

"No."

"I thought there was such a thing as discovery," Aaron said.

"There is. And I can't wait to see what surprise evidence they 'discover' once the trial begins."

"Chief Harper will tip you off."

"Ordinarily, yes. At the moment, he'd like to keep his job." Cora took a messy bite of taco. Ground beef and melted cheese dripped down her sleeve. She saw it, quoted Henry Firth.

"Watch your mouth," Sherry said. "No one's bleeping you."

"Relax, she's eating tacos."

"Tacos!"

"See?" Sherry said.

"Unpause the TV," Cora said. "I wanna see how I did."

"You never cared how you did on TV," Sherry said.

"I was never concerned with the jury pool before."

The phone rang. Cora went in the kitchen, picked it up.

It was Becky Baldwin. "I got the witness list."

"And?"

"No surprises. You got the cops, you got the medical examiner, you got the hotel clerk. You got Paula Martindale."

"Kill me now."

"And they got the crossword puzzle on your machine."

"It's a strong case, but not a convicting case," Cora said. "They need something else. Like my fingerprints on the knife."

"You left your fingerprints on the knife?"

"Of course not."

"When Paula Martindale dropped it, you didn't pick it up?"

"Absolutely not."

"It's a natural reaction. You're confronted by a distraught woman holding a deadly weapon. Disarming her is a number-one priority."

"She disarmed herself."

"She dropped the knife on the floor, and then what did you do with it?"

"I didn't do anything."

"You went in and looked at the body?"

"Yeah."

"Leaving Paula Martindale there with the knife?"

"No, I took her with me."

"Why?"

"What do you mean, why?" Cora said irritably. "What else was I going to do with her? I couldn't leave her there with the knife, could I?"

"See?" Becky said. "These are the kind of questions they're going to throw at you to try to make you look bad to the jury. Getting you angry is just the first step."

"Thanks for calling. You've made my day. Can I go back to my tacos?"

"You're having tacos?"

"Sorry. I would have invited you, but Sherry gets jealous."

"She does not. That's one of those stories you make up out of whole cloth."

"I don't know what you're talking about," Cora said. She hung up the phone, went back in the living room.

"What's up?" Sherry said.

"Becky Baldwin wants to have tacos with Aaron."

CHAPTER 38

Henry Firth smiled at the jury.

"It takes a big man to admit when he's wrong. As you all know, just last week I was trying someone else for the murder of Roger Martindale. His wife, Paula Martindale, was accused of the crime. And there was certainly plenty of evidence against her. As you will learn, during the course of this trial, that evidence was carefully manufactured by the defendant, Cora Felton, to frame Paula Martindale for the crime. I, like everyone else, was taken in by the evidence and believed that Paula Martindale was guilty.

"Then new evidence came to light.

"The prosecution expects to show that the defendant, Cora Felton, had been having an affair with Roger Martindale. For the past month they had been having afternoon trysts at a midtown Manhattan hotel. We expect to show that Paula Martindale had become suspicious of her husband, and, in a scenario straight out of the movies, drove to Manhattan, staked out his office building, and waited in the shadows for him to come out. Sure enough, in the early afternoon Roger Martindale came out of the building, hopped in a cab, and went straight to the Fifty-seventh Street hotel. Paula Martindale followed him to the hotel and waited to see who would join him.

"Unfortunately for her, the defendant, Cora Felton, had worked as a private investigator and was not without her own detecting skills. So Cora Felton saw Paula Martindale before Paula saw her.

"You can imagine how the defendant felt. Here she is, sneaking off to meet her lover, and there's his wife at the hotel, spying on him.

"Naturally, Cora did not go up to the room. She called Roger Martindale, told him his wife was watching him, and made herself scarce.

"Well, you can imagine how Roger Martindale felt. His wife was on to him. She'd discovered his infidelity and was looking to catch him at it. Naturally, he did the only thing possible. He told Cora Felton he would have to break it off."

Henry Firth held up one finger. "Not a

good move on his part. There is nothing more dangerous than a woman scorned. One can only imagine the tears and recriminations that would have resulted. And, as so often happens in these cases, a lover becomes a liability. A lead weight around her lover's neck. A threat to break up his marriage, which is something Roger Martindale never intended.

"And Roger Martindale, torn between a suspicious wife and a clingy, nagging lover, ran kicking and screaming straight into the arms of another woman. He went out after work, got drunk, picked up a woman, and, for the first time in his life, simply didn't come home.

"Well, you can imagine what his wife thought: He's with his lover. But Paula spoiled their matinees, so he scheduled an evening performance.

"If only it were true.

"Paula Martindale was hysterical. She went to the police, but they couldn't help her because it hadn't been twenty-four hours. In an ironic twist of fate, Chief Harper, unable to act himself, asked Cora Felton to deal with Paula Martindale.

"Cora Felton was astounded. It was the first she'd heard anything about it. Roger Martindale was missing? He hadn't come home? So she went out to talk to Paula. What a conversation that must have been! Two nearly hysterical women, wondering what had happened to their man. Both suspected a lover. But only Cora Felton knew it was *another* lover.

"Nothing comes of the meeting. Paula refuses to entertain the idea her husband might have a lover. She insists it isn't true. Cora knows she's lying, having seen her at the hotel, but of course she can't say anything. She's very upset, and she's relieved just to get through the meeting.

"What happens next? Chief Harper calls Cora Felton at home. It's been over twenty-four hours and Roger Martindale is now an official missing person. He asks Cora to come to his office and discuss the case.

"She does, but not right away. She takes her time getting there. Chief Harper even comments on the fact. Where was she during that forty-five minutes to an hour? She was meeting her lover, demanding an explanation, and stabbing him to death in a fit of jealous rage.

"We expect to show that Cora Felton tricked Paula Martindale into leaving the house. And how did she do that? With a crossword puzzle, no less! A crossword puzzle, the original of which was subsequently discovered by the police in Cora Felton's crossword puzzle–constructing program on Cora Felton's own personal computer!

"As soon as Paula Martindale was out of the way, Cora Felton snuck into the house and armed herself with a butcher knife from the kitchen. When Roger Martindale came slinking in with his tail between his legs, still drunk and hungover from binging on alcohol and drugs, Cora Felton ambushed him and struck him down, leaving his bloody corpse lying on the living room rug.

"She ran out and raced to the police station to keep her appointment with Chief Harper. Her intention was to manipulate the chief into going out to the house. They would find Roger Martindale dead and Paula Martindale gone. It would look like Paula Martindale fled.

"Luck was with her. No sooner did she arrive at the police station when Officer Dan Finley got a report that Roger Martindale had picked up his car from a garage near his office. Chief Harper called Paula to tell her, got no answer, and decided to drive out there.

"Cora Felton went with him. Doubtless she intended to contrive to get blood on her clothes, so she would have an excuse in case some had splattered when she stabbed Roger dead.

"Luck was with her again. Paula Martindale had just returned home and found her husband lying on the floor in a pool of blood. She fell to her knees in a frenzy, trying to revive him, and pulled the knife from his chest. She heard the front door and sprang up in a panic, thinking it might be the killer.

"It was!"

The jurors were on the edge of their seats. Some actually jumped.

Henry Firth smiled. "But she didn't know it." He chuckled ironically at his little joke. "Because it wasn't an armed man threatening to harm her. It was merely Cora Felton and Chief Harper, come to tell her that her husband had been found. And Paula Martindale still had no idea Cora Felton was her husband's secret lover, let alone the person who had taken his life.

"For Cora Felton, it couldn't have been better. Paula Martindale had just pulled the knife from her husband's body, and she was holding it when she met them in the foyer. Perhaps she had it for her protection; more likely, she didn't even realize it was in her hand. She didn't react when Chief Harper told her to drop it, not even when he drew

244

his gun.

"Cora Felton saw her chance. She grabbed Paula, twisted the knife out of her hand, and subdued her in a bear hug, conveniently smearing blood all over herself."

Henry Firth spread his arms, shrugged his shoulders. "It was as simple as that." He paused a moment to let that sink in, then raised a finger for emphasis. "This was no accident, ladies and gentlemen. This was no act of self-defense. This was not even a crime committed in the heat of passion. Cora Felton manipulated Paula Martindale out of the house, armed herself with a butcher knife, and lay in wait for her husband. This was a cold-blooded, premeditated murder. We will prove this beyond a shadow of a doubt, and we shall expect a verdict of guilty at your hands."

Henry Firth bowed to the jury, strode back to the prosecution table, and sat down with a huge smile of satisfaction on his face.

CHAPTER 39

Becky Baldwin smiled at the jurors.

"Ladies and gentlemen of the jury, I know the prosecutor is waiting for me to say something, like how it takes a big man to be wrong and a bigger man to be wrong twice. But I'm not going to do that. Because there is another part of his opening statement I am much more concerned with."

Just as Henry Firth had done, Becky raised one finger for emphasis. "Do you know how many times the prosecutor used the phrase 'you can only imagine'? I don't, because I lost count after the first four or five. He seemed to say it every other phrase. And he's absolutely right. You can only imagine. And the reason you can only imagine is because he doesn't know. He has no facts. No evidence. No witnesses. Just idle speculation. If you listen to his entire case, you will find that the only reason at all that he thinks Cora Felton did it is because now he thinks Paula Martindale didn't. By the same reasoning, I must have won the presidential election because Paula Martindale didn't. Well, ladies and gentlemen, much as I hate to disillusion you, I am not the president of the United States. I am Cora Felton's attorney, which is a much easier job. I don't even have to deal with Congress. All I have to do is listen to the prosecutor put on his case and when he's done, say, 'Is that all you've got? Bring in your verdict and let's go to lunch.' "

Becky smiled. "I just hope he doesn't drag it out too long. I'm kind of hungry."

CHAPTER 40

Henry Firth rather quickly breezed through the same witnesses he'd used in the first trial — the cops, the medical examiner — asking virtually the same questions he'd asked before. It was only when he recalled Officer Dan Finley that things got interesting.

Dan seemed rather reluctant to take the stand.

Cora nudged Becky. "That's not good."

"Shhh!"

"Officer Finley," Henry Firth said, "you testified to searching Roger Martindale's body and inventorying the items you found on his person?"

"Yes, I did."

"When you searched the body, did you find his cell phone?"

"No, it was not on the body."

"Did you subsequently find it?"

"Yes, I did."

"Where was it?"

"Under the front seat of his car."

"Do you have that cell phone here in court?"

"Yes, I do."

Dan Finley took out a plastic evidence bag with a cell phone in it.

"Is this the cell phone that you found?"

"Yes, it is."

"How do you identify it?"

"I placed it in this evidence bag and wrote my name on it. The phone is also registered to Roger Martindale and has his phone number."

"I ask the cell phone be marked for identification."

"No objection."

"So ordered."

"Officer Finley, did you trace the phone calls received by that cell phone on the day of Roger Martindale's death?"

"Yes. There were no phone calls received on that date."

"Were there any missed calls?"

"Yes, there were four."

"For the benefit of those jurors who might not be cell phone savvy, what are 'missed calls'?"

"Calls that were not picked up. The calls came into the phone but were not answered."

"And who were the missed calls from?"

Dan said it grudgingly. He couldn't meet Cora's eyes. "Cora Felton."

"I beg your pardon," Henry Firth said. "Did you say the phone calls were from Cora Felton?"

"That's right."

"And how many calls were there?"

"Four."

"All from Cora Felton?"

"Yes."

"The decedent received four separate phone calls from Cora Felton on the day of his death?"

"He didn't receive *any* calls. There were several calls he didn't answer."

"Four of them, all from the defendant, Cora Felton?"

Judge Hobbs stirred restlessly. "Ms. Baldwin. These questions would seem to have been already asked and answered."

"Your Honor," Becky said. "The prosecutor plainly intends to smear my client by insinuation and innuendo. By pretending to be balked by technical objections, he can make it look like we have something to hide. The defense has nothing to hide. If he has any evidence, bring it on. Though, as I mentioned, I would like to get out of here by lunch."

The remark drew a laugh.

Judge Hobbs banged the gavel.

Becky smiled. "I'm sorry, Your Honor. I should have said that at the sidebar."

"As there is no objection, you may proceed, Mr. Firth."

"Thank you, Your Honor. Officer Finley, on any of those missed calls, did the defendant leave a message?"

Dan Finley shook his head. "No. Then they wouldn't have been missed calls. They'd have been logged in the in-box."

"And that didn't happen?"

"No."

"There were no calls in the in-box?"

"No."

"How about *outgoing* calls? Did Roger Martindale *make* any calls on the day of his death?"

"Yes, he did."

"How many calls?"

"One."

"And who was that call to?"

Once again, Dan couldn't meet Cora's eyes. "Cora Felton."

"Roger Martindale called Cora Felton?"

"That's right."

"And was that call answered?"

"Yes, it was."

"How long did that call last?"

"A minute and forty-five seconds."

"So there was no doubt that call was picked up?"

"It went through."

"And that call was to the defendant, Cora Felton?"

"That's right."

"And that was the only call Roger Martindale made on the day of his death?"

"That's right."

"One more thing, Officer Finley: Can you tell me the time of that phone call from Roger Martindale to the defendant?"

"Yes. It was at five forty-five."

"Within an hour of the time Roger Martindale met his death?"

"I'm not a medical examiner."

"I understand. No further questions."

"Any cross-examination, Ms. Baldwin?"

"Frankly, I'm not sure, Your Honor. If I might have a brief recess?"

"A recess, Your Honor?" Henry Firth said. "I thought the defense attorney was concerned with getting to lunch."

Judge Hobbs put up his hand. "That will do, Mr. Firth. Ms. Baldwin, it's not as if you have to locate a witness. You can have a short recess. Ten minutes, keep it to fifteen."

Chapter 41

Becky hustled Cora into a small conference room.

"Gee, you were good," Cora said. "What was that 'insinuation and innuendo' bit?"

"Read it in a Perry Mason book. I had to say something."

"You did fine."

"Stop stalling. What about the phone calls?"

"What phone calls? Roger didn't get any phone calls."

"Because you missed him and he didn't answer."

"Well, if you want to hold me accountable for things that didn't happen . . ."

"Cora, I don't have time for your word games. What about his call to you?"

"Never happened."

"It was answered."

"Not by me."

"You're saying someone else picked up

your phone?"

"They couldn't have. I was at home."

"Then you got the call."

"But I didn't."

"Are you sure?"

"I don't think I'd forget something like that."

"What if you did?"

"What do you mean?"

"What if you *did* get the phone call? The phone records say you did. So either you're lying to me, or you don't know you got it. If you're lying to me, it's one thing, but if you didn't get it, that's another. If you got it and you don't know it, how could that have happened?"

"It couldn't."

"Did you get any calls at all?"

"Chief Harper. Asking me to come to the station."

"Besides that."

"How the hell should I know?"

"Well, concentrate. You should recall answering the phone. Because Roger Martindale is missing, and you're expecting the call about him. And you'll pick up the phone for anyone, because you don't have Caller ID."

"I don't want Caller ID. I want to pick up the phone and get someone."

"So if the phone rang you'd have picked it up."

"All right."

"So did the phone ring?"

"Becky —"

"Come on, think. You're waiting for the call about Roger Martindale. If you got a call that *wasn't* about Roger Martindale, it would be annoying. So do you remember getting calls that were annoying?"

"I always get calls that are annoying. I . . ."

"You remember something?"

"I got a call from one of those scam artists. You know, 'Your computer has a virus, let me fix it for you.' I offered to fix certain parts of his anatomy for him until he realized I wasn't going to give him my credit card number and hung up."

"That was it?"

"Yeah."

"What time was that?"

"How the hell should I know?"

"That was the call."

"What?"

"That was the call from Roger Martindale. Someone is framing you for the murder. They need a record of Roger Martindale calling you from his cell phone on the night of the murder. So whoever killed Roger Martindale took his cell phone, called you up, and pretended to be a computer scammer." Becky frowned. "Except for one thing."

"What's that?"

"Then the killer was a man."

"Or a woman disguising her voice," Cora said.

"Is that possible?"

"Of course it is. It was a high-pitched, foreign-sounding voice. Which is not surprising. Half the people in India want to fix my computer."

"Okay, that's gotta be it. Good. We can deal with this at the proper time. I'll go easy on Dan. He still looks like a little boy, and the jury won't like me if I pick on him."

Cora shook her head. "Jeez, has it really come to that?'

"Cora, it's not good. But we can handle this." Becky smiled grimly. "Let's just hope they don't have anything else."

CHAPTER 42

When court reconvened, Judge Hobbs said, "When we broke for recess, Officer Finley was on the stand, and Mr. Firth had just completed his direct examination. Ms. Baldwin, do you wish to cross-examine?"

"Just a few questions, Your Honor. Officer Finley, you testified at the previous murder trial, when Paula Martindale was being tried for the crime?"

"That's right."

"And you described what was found at the crime scene. I don't recall you mentioning a cell phone."

"No, we hadn't found it at the time. It had slipped out of Roger Martindale's pocket and become wedged between the driver's seat and the gearshift column of his car."

"How did you come to discover it?"

"Actually, his wife found it, cleaning out his car for sale. She brought it to the police."

"Thank you, Officer Finley. That's all."

Henry Firth declined redirect.

"The witness is excused. Call your next witness."

"Call Paula Martindale."

The courtroom was abuzz as Paula Martindale took the stand. It was almost surreal for Cora and Becky to watch the woman they had been working for sworn in.

Henry Firth didn't mince words. "You're Paula Martindale?"

"That's right."

"You were married to the decedent, Roger Martindale?"

"Yes, I was."

"You were once accused of the murder of your husband, Roger Martindale?"

"Yes."

"How did that happen?"

"It wasn't the fault of the police. I was manipulated into a position where it looked like I had done it."

"You were set up?"

"Yes, I was."

"In what way?"

"My husband had been missing for over twenty-four hours. He had been placed on the missing persons list. I didn't know what happened. All I could think of was that he had been kidnapped. I was waiting for a ransom demand. It never came. Instead I got a crossword puzzle."

"Excuse me," Henry Firth said. "I want to be sure I understand this. You say you got a crossword puzzle?"

"That's right."

"How did you get it?"

"It was left on my doorstep."

"When?"

Paula shook her head. "I have no idea. I'd been in the house all day, waiting to hear something. I was pacing nervously. I went to the front door, looked out. It was lying on the stoop."

"What time was this?"

"Around five thirty. It was a printed puzzle, you know, like it was generated by computer. There was writing on the top."

"What did it say?"

"It said, 'Go to the Bakerhaven mall at six o'clock, park in front of Walmart, roll down your window, stick your hand out, and burn this puzzle.' "

"It told you to burn the puzzle?"

"Yes."

"Why?"

"I don't know. I assume as a signal that I was going along, doing what I was told."

"What did you do?"

"First, I solved the puzzle."

"Why?"

"To see if there was a clue. I figured there had to be a reason the kidnapper used a puzzle. It certainly wasn't the most convenient piece of paper to use. He had to write along the edge, where there wasn't much room. So I thought it might say something."

"Did it?"

"Yes. There was a short poem. Suggesting my husband might have been involved with another woman."

"What did you think of that?"

"I didn't believe it. I figured it was a trick to keep me from knowing what was really going on."

"What did you do then?"

"Just what it said. I hopped in my car, drove to the mall, and parked in front of Walmart. I rolled down my window and burned the puzzle."

"What happened then?"

"Nothing. I sat there waiting, and nothing happened. Finally, I gave up and went home."

Cora sucked in her breath. This was bad. Very bad. The jurors were on the edge of their seats, waiting to hear what the witness said.

"And what did you find when you got there?"

"Roger's car was out front. I was delighted. Suddenly, it all didn't matter. The crossword puzzle, the mall, the stupid instructions. My husband was home. I rushed up the walk, went inside, called his name. There was no answer. I went in the living room, and . . . and . . ." She turned her head away.

Henry Firth couldn't have been more sympathetic. "I understand this is hard for you, but we need to know. Take your time, and tell us what you saw."

Paula Martindale looked up. Her lip trembled. It occurred to Cora if she was acting, it was a terrific job.

"He was on the living room floor. There was blood everywhere. He was lying on a white rug, and the splatters —" Her voice caught. She looked away. "I can't."

"Take your time."

"May I have some water, please?"

The bailiff filled a glass with water, handed it to the witness. She took a sip, gagged, choked, gulped it down. She exhaled sharply as if she'd been holding her breath, then breathed in and out as if to calm herself.

She extended the glass back to the bailiff. Composed herself. Looked up at Henry Firth expectantly.

"You were telling us about finding your

husband," he prompted. He said it so softly, Cora had to strain to hear. She recognized the tactic. It was so quiet in the courtroom you could hear a pin drop. He was merely underlining the fact.

Paula shuddered slightly. She gripped the arms of the witness stand, steeled herself, forged ahead. "Roger was on the floor, covered with blood. A big knife was sticking out of his stomach. I knelt by him, held his head, spoke to him. I told him to wake up. He . . . he wasn't breathing. I grabbed the knife. Pulled it out of his stomach." She closed her eyes, swallowed, opened them again. "Blood gushed out. I had a flash of fear, a sudden icy doubt that somehow I'd made it worse. That he would die, and it would be my fault.

"I heard the sound of the doorbell. Help. I needed help. I lunged to my feet, ran to the foyer.

"It was Chief Harper and Cora Felton. I said, 'Something happened to Roger!' I expected them to help me. They didn't. Chief Harper told me to put down the knife. I didn't know what he was talking about. I didn't know why he wasn't running to help. I just looked at him.

"Then he drew his gun.

"I couldn't believe it. I thought he'd lost

his mind. I thought *I'd* lost my mind. Nothing made any sense.

"Cora Felton walked up to me, grabbed my arm. It took me a minute to realize what she was doing. I started to pull away. She twisted, hard. I heard something clatter on the floor. I looked, saw the knife.

"Cora Felton spun me around, held me tight."

"What happened then?"

"Chief Harper took me into custody."

"Thank you, Mrs. Martindale." Henry Firth turned to the defense table. His eyes locked with Becky Baldwin's. "Your witness."

Cora knew what the prosecutor was doing. Having presented the witness in such a sympathetic light, with the sobs and the water, he was *daring* Becky Baldwin to attack her.

Becky knew what he was doing, too. She hesitated a moment.

"Ms. Baldwin," Judge Hobbs prompted. "Does the defense have any questions for the witness?"

Becky rose to her feet.

"The defense does, Your Honor."

Chapter 43

Becky took her time approaching the witness. "Mrs. Martindale, I realize this is difficult for you, but I need to go over your statement just to be sure I understand everything. With regard to the crossword puzzle you found. You say it was left on your doorstep?"

"That's right."

"When you found it, what made you think it had to do with your husband's disappearance?"

"The message on the top. Telling me to go to the mall."

"Did it mention your husband?"

"Not specifically. It just said those were my instructions and I should follow them to the letter."

"And the instructions were to go to the mall and burn the puzzle?"

"Yes."

"Which you did."

"That's right."

"Since you burned it, you have no evidence you ever received it."

"That's not true. The police found a copy of the puzzle."

"How do you know?"

"They told me. They showed me the puzzle."

"How do you know it's the same puzzle?"

"It had the same message."

"The same *exact* message?"

"I think so."

"And what was that message?"

Paula Martindale took a breath. " 'Wanna know where he is? Wooing her with a kiss.' "

"You remembered it word for word?"

"Not at the time. I've learned it now."

"You learned it from the puzzle the police showed you?"

"Yes."

"But you didn't know it when they first showed it to you."

"I knew it generally. And it certainly seemed the same."

"You were on trial for this crime?"

"Yes."

"The charges against you were dismissed on the basis of this puzzle you claim you burned at the mall."

"The charges were dismissed because I

didn't do it."

"I understand your contention. But the reason the prosecutor reached that conclusion was on the strength of your alibi that you burned the crossword puzzle at the mall at the time of the crime. You described a crossword puzzle. A similar crossword puzzle was established to exist, giving some basis to your story of burning one. Which doesn't mean you did."

"Is the defense attorney asking a question or making an argument?" Henry Firth said.

"Is it or is it not true that the only evidence that you burned *anything* at the mall at the time of the murder is your unsubstantiated story?"

"No, it is not."

Becky frowned. "It is not?"

"No. I have witnesses."

"Witnesses?"

"People saw me do it."

"You now claim you have witnesses to the fact you burned something at the mall?"

"That's right."

"When you were my client, did you ever tell *me* you had witnesses to the fact you burned something at the mall?"

"Objection, Your Honor. How is anything the witness may have told her former attorney possibly relevant?"

"Sustained."

"May I be heard, Your Honor?" Becky said.

"At the sidebar."

Becky and Henry Firth moved to the sidebar to confer with the judge out of earshot of the jury.

"Your Honor," Becky said, "the witness is attempting to bolster her story with the claim that people actually saw her do it. I think the fact that it's just now that it occurs to her that there were witnesses to the event is entirely relevant."

"And you're entitled to your opinion," Judge Hobbs said. "However, what the witness may or may not have told you is clearly *not* relevant. If you wish to make that point, make it another way. Step back."

Becky and the prosecutor resumed their positions.

"Mrs. Martindale, with regard to these witnesses you now claim saw you at the mall: Who might they be?"

"Ken Jessup. He walked right by me. Just as I was about to burn the puzzle."

"The hell I did!"

Heads turned.

In the middle of the gallery, Ken Jessup had lunged to his feet to glare at the witness.

Judge Hobbs banged the gavel. "Order! Order in the court! Mr. Jessup, hold your tongue and sit down!"

"But she's lying, Your Honor!"

"Silence! Another word and you'll be in contempt of court!"

"Who, me? She's the one —"

"Bailiff! Remove this man!"

The bailiff pushed through the gate and took hold of Jessup's arm. Jessup twisted away.

"Chief Harper: Would you assist the bailiff?"

Dan Finley was already on his feet. The three men converged on Ken Jessup, who put up his hands. "Hold on! Hold on! This isn't necessary. I'll be quiet."

"A little late for that, Mr. Jessup. Bailiff?"

A rather chastened Ken Jessup was led out.

Becky Baldwin watched him go, then turned back to Paula Martindale with an ironic smile. "*That's* your witness?"

"He saw me. He may not want to admit it, but he walked right by me just as I was about to burn the puzzle."

"Are you sure?"

"Absolutely. He was a friend of my husband. I wanted to ask him if he'd seen him. I started to get out of my car. I stopped myself. I realized I shouldn't. The kidnapper must be watching to see if I burned the puzzle. I pulled my head back in the window and he went on by. But I'm sure he saw me."

"But he didn't see you burn a puzzle?"

"No."

"He just saw you sitting in a car in front of Walmart."

"That's right."

"Then he would have no reason to remember the incident."

"Except that it's important."

"It wasn't important then."

"No, but my husband was missing. He must have thought it odd I was sitting alone in a car with my husband missing."

"You're saying it would have made an impression on him and he would remember it?"

"I believe so."

"Clearly, it didn't."

"Clearly, it did. He may deny it because he doesn't want to help me, but it's true."

"If I might have a moment, Your Honor." Becky walked over to the defense table, looked through her papers. She selected one, said, "Your Honor, I ask this be marked for identification as Defense Exhibit A."

"So ordered."

When the paper had been marked for

identification, Becky handed it to the witness. "Mrs. Martindale, I handed you a piece of paper. Do you know what this is?"

"It's a list of names."

"That's right. Do you know what discovery is? With regard to courtroom procedure?"

"No, I don't."

"The prosecution has to tell the defense what witnesses they intend to call. So we can be prepared for them. This is a list of the prosecution's witnesses in this case."

"If you say so."

"Your name is on the list."

"That's right."

"Do you see the name Ken Jessup?"

Paula scanned the list. "No, I do not."

"Mrs. Martindale, have you discussed your testimony with the prosecutor, Henry Firth?"

"Yes, of course."

"Did you tell him you had witnesses to burning a puzzle at the mall?"

"Yes, I did."

"Wouldn't you think if Ken Jessup really had seen you at the mall, his name would be on this list?"

"Objection, Your Honor. Is defense counsel asking questions or making an argument?"

"Sustained. You've made your point, Ms. Baldwin. Move it along."

"Yes, Your Honor. Well, Mrs. Martindale, that's one witness. Who are the others?"

"I don't know."

"You don't know?" Becky said ironically. "Then it's no wonder *their* names aren't on the list."

That sally drew an appreciative murmur of amusement.

"Lots of people went by. I can't remember who. I remember him because he was a friend of my husband. But no one else made an impression. You have to understand: I was distraught. I was thinking of my husband. If Ken Jessup hadn't been his friend, I wouldn't have noticed *him*. He went by. I almost talked to him. I was angry at myself that I didn't. I kept vacillating: 'I should talk to him. No, I shouldn't.' I wished I had. When he drove out, I even thought about stopping his car. But I was about to burn the puzzle, and —" She sucked in her breath. "Oh! The old man!"

"What old man?"

"An old man stumbled in front of Ken's car. He almost hit him. He had to swerve to avoid him."

"So?"

"He saw me."

271

"The old man?"

"Yes."

"And who was this old man?"

"I don't know his name. He was just an old man."

"Is he in the courtroom?"

Paula scanned the crowd. "No, he is not."

"Why am I not surprised," Becky said.

"Oh, Your Honor . . ." Henry Firth said.

"Exactly," Judge Hobbs said. "Ms. Baldwin, if you would keep your editorial comments to yourself."

"Yes, Your Honor." Becky turned back to the witness, smiled broadly. "So, Ken Jessup is the *only* witness you can produce who saw you in that parking lot?"

"Yes."

"No further questions."

There was a shocked gasp from the courtroom, followed by the buzz of voices.

With a frozen smile plastered on her face, Cora murmured out of the corner of her mouth, "What the hell are you doing?"

"Tell you during recess."

"I can't wait until recess."

"Don't think you'll have to."

"Any redirect?" Judge Hobbs said.

Henry Firth stood up. "Frankly, I'm not sure, Your Honor. If I might have a short recess?"

"Very well. Ten minutes. Court is in recess."

CHAPTER 44

Cora managed not to explode until they were alone in the conference room. "Are you out of your mind? That's a key prosecution witness. She just told a wild fairy story about finding her husband murdered. The only reason she's telling it is the prosecution has to account for the fact she was found clutching a bloody knife. It's a gore-dripped horror story any third-grade kid would be embarrassed to have made up. But do you challenge it? Not at all. Instead you make a big deal about the crossword puzzle. Which is the last thing in the world we want to emphasize. It may seem stupid as hell I would use a crossword puzzle in a plot to kill someone, but that doesn't mean twelve moronic jurors won't take it at face value and decide I must have done it. Particularly when it's been planted on my computer."

"You make a good point."

"I make a good point? What do you mean,

I make a good point? I don't want to make a good point. I want you to tear that slimy, lying bitch a new one."

"No, you don't."

Cora's mouth fell open. "Now you're telling me what I *want*?"

"No, I'm telling you what you need. You need Paula Martindale's testimony not to crucify you. Which it is very apt to do. Did you see the faces of the jurors as she told her story? They were lapping it up. They couldn't wait to hear what she was going to say next." Becky put up her hand. "Yes, I could tear her apart. How do you think the jury's going to feel about that? Every question I ask just makes it worse. This poor, wronged woman, confronted with her bloody, dying husband. You want to give her a few more chances to stutter, sob, drink a glass of water? Not only does it paint a sympathetic picture of her, but they'll hate me for it. And if they hate me, they hate you."

"So you let her get away."

"But I didn't. I nailed her on the witnesses. That's not just for show. Burning the puzzle is her alibi. That's what puts her at the mall instead of home, stabbing her husband. If her alibi holds up, we're sunk. That's why I'm making a big deal of it.

Everything I said in court was true. Henry Firth's got a problem with the alibi witnesses. There *are* none. If her alibi falls apart, we've got the reasonable doubt we need to win this case."

Cora looked at Becky. "That's what it's come to? Reasonable doubt?"

"You were hoping for a courtroom confession?"

"No, of course not. But I was hoping for a reasonable explanation."

"Me, too. But I'll take an unreasonable one if I can't get it. Right now I'm trying to break the prosecutor's flow and force him to put Ken Jessup on the stand."

"Why would he? You saw him in court. He's obviously a bad witness. He was Roger Martindale's friend. He thought his wife killed him. He probably still does. At any rate, he hates her a lot. He's not going to back up her alibi, and he may blow it up."

"Yeah. If the prosecutor doesn't call him, I will. But then he's a rebuttal witness. If he discredits her story as a prosecution witness, that's gold. That's why I'm daring Henry Firth to put him on the stand. You know it, I know it, the judge knows it, and everyone in the courtroom knows it. If Henry Firth doesn't call him now, it will look like he doesn't dare. And the pendulum swings in our favor."

"Good God," Cora said. "Did you really say 'the pendulum swings in our favor'?"

"Sorry," Becky said. "This case is getting to me."

"It's getting to *you*?"

"Anyway, Ken Jessup is a bully and coward. You saw how quickly he caved when the bailiff showed up. So did Henry Firth. He's working on him now. If Jessup holds out on him, which I'm hoping he will, Henry Firth won't dare put him on the stand."

Becky checked her watch. "Well, recess is almost over. This will tell the story. If Henry Firth asks questions on redirect, trying to suck me into questioning Paula about finding the body, we'll know his case is shaky, that Ken Jessup isn't going to do him any good. Then we're in business."

"What if he calls him to the stand?"

"Then we're screwed."

CHAPTER 45

When court reconvened Judge Hobbs said, "Now then, the witness Paula Martindale was on the stand and Ms. Baldwin had just completed her cross-examination. Mr. Firth, do you have any redirect?"

"No, Your Honor."

"Very well. The witness is excused. Call your next witness."

"Call Ken Jessup."

Becky and Cora exchanged glances.

"Should I write my will?" Cora said.

"Shhh."

A rather contrite-looking Ken Jessup was led in and took the stand.

Henry Firth approached him. "Your name is Ken Jessup?"

"Yes."

"Did you know Roger Martindale in his lifetime?"

"Yes. I was his friend."

"Did you know his wife, Paula Martin-dale?"

"Yes. She is *not* my friend."

"But you knew her on sight?"

"Yes, of course."

"Directing your attention to the day Roger Martindale was killed: Were you at the mall that day?"

"I have no idea."

"You have no idea?"

"It's a long time ago. I don't remember."

"It *was* a particular day. I'm sure you remember getting the news Roger had been killed. Wouldn't that heighten your memory with regard to where you were that day, and when?"

"Perhaps. But I don't remember."

"Mr. Jessup, on the witness stand Paula Martindale testified that she was sitting in a parked car outside of Walmart and you looked at her face."

"I am not responsible for what Paula Martindale may or may not have testified. But I know she wasn't at the mall that night."

"How do you know that?"

"Because she was home killing her husband."

Henry Firth smiled grimly. "Permission to treat the witness as hostile, Your Honor?"

"Granted."

"Mr. Jessup, on the day you heard Roger Martindale had been killed, did you know that he'd been missing?"

The witness hesitated.

"If you were a friend of his, I would think you had. It had been over twenty-four hours. He'd been placed on the missing persons list. So if you saw his wife sitting alone in a parked car with the window down at a shopping mall, wouldn't you think it had something to do with his disappearance?"

Ken Jessup took a breath, glowered at the prosecutor.

"Mr. Jessup?"

"You're the one making that connection, not me."

"Let me put it this way, Mr. Jessup. You claim you didn't see Paula Martindale sitting alone in a parked car at the mall on the evening of his husband's murder. Did you *ever* see Paula Martindale sitting alone in a parked car at the mall in front of Walmart?"

Ken Jessup's eyes shifted.

"Oh? You remember something?"

"I remember seeing her sitting in a parked car in the parking lot. But I *don't* recall what night it was."

"But you recall the incident? You walked by. She was looking out the window. She looked straight at you. And you looked straight at her."

"You're making too much of it."

"Did it happen, yes or no?"

"Yes, it happened. But I have no idea when."

"According to Paula Martindale, you walked by just before she burned a crossword puzzle. On the occasion you remember, did Paula Martindale burn anything?"

"No, she did not."

"Did she stick anything out the window?"

"Her head."

Laughter rocked the courtroom. Henry Firth waited until it subsided, said, "Aside from that. Did she stick her arm out? Did she stick out her hand with anything in it?"

"If she did, I didn't see it."

"After you walked past her car, what did you do?'

"Got in my car and went home."

"On your way out of the parking lot, did you drive past Paula Martindale's car?"

"I must have."

"Did you see her sitting there?"

"I have no recollection of seeing her at all."

"As you drove by her car, did you see an old man in the road?"

Ken Jessup's eyes shifted.

"You remember now?"

"No, I don't remember now."

"You reacted to my question about the old man."

"I reacted to the words 'old man.' Because of a separate incident. I was driving out of the parking lot and an old man staggered in front of my car. I had to slow down and wait for him to get out of the way."

"As you were passing Paula Martindale's car?'

"I have no idea where and when it happened. I only know it happened driving out of the parking lot. I don't think the one thing had anything to do with the other. But when you mention an old man walking in front of my car, that's the image that I see."

"Is that old man in the courtroom?"

"No, he's not."

"Do you know his name?"

"I don't know his name. I've seen him around town. I don't want to slander anyone, but it occurs to me he might have occasionally had a drink or two. That was undoubtedly the case when he lurched in front of my car."

"Would that be Luke Haslett?"

Jessup frowned. "I believe that's his name."

Henry Firth turned to the judge. "Your Honor: In view of the testimony of this witness, I would ask for an adjournment until tomorrow to allow me to locate this witness, Luke Haslett."

"No objection, Your Honor," Becky said.

"Very well. Court is adjourned until ten tomorrow."

CHAPTER 46

Luke Haslett did not look like the ideal witness. Red, bleary eyes, runny nose, scraggly hair, unshaven face. His teeth were yellow and crooked. One was missing, an upper molar, close enough to the front to provide an unattractive gap. His clothes were rumpled and dirty, his shirt untucked, his zipper only half up. Sitting there in the prosecutor's office, he looked like a trapped rat.

Henry Firth regarded him with distaste. "Mr. Haslett, do you know why you're here?"

"Got arrested."

"You're not arrested, Mr. Haslett."

"I can go?"

"We want to ask you a few questions."

"I'm not under arrest?"

"You're not under arrest."

"If I'm under arrest I don't have to answer questions. That's the law."

"Yes, Mr. Haslett. But you're not under

arrest. You didn't do anything wrong."

"I can go?"

"You can't go. You're a witness."

Haslett's forehead crinkled into a frown. "Huh?"

"We're not asking about what you *did*. We're asking about what you *saw.*"

"Didn't see nothing."

Henry Firth took a deep breath. He couldn't believe what a long shot this was becoming. "Mr. Haslett, were you ever at the Bakerhaven mall?"

"Didn't do nothing."

"No one says you did. Do you remember walking through the parking lot?"

"Whole mall's a parking lot."

"Mr. Haslett, do you know Paula Martindale?"

"Who?"

"Paula Martindale. Her husband was killed."

"Didn't do it!"

"We know you didn't do it. It's his wife we're talking about. Paula Martindale. She was sitting in a car at the mall. Do you remember walking by the car and seeing her sitting there?"

"Don't know who she is."

Henry Firth's heart sank. "Mr. Haslett, did a car almost hit you?"

"Damn driver!"

"A driver almost hit you?"

"Yelled at him."

"You remember the car? What kind of car was it?"

Haslett's brow furrowed furiously in concentration. He nodded his head. "Burning."

Henry Firth's mouth fell open. He was almost afraid to ask the question, not wanting to break the spell. "Something was burning?"

Haslett nodded, more to himself than in answer to the question.

"Paper."

CHAPTER 47

Crowley scooped up the phone in his office. "Crowley," he growled.

"Felton," Cora growled back.

"Sorry," Crowley said. "Expecting some calls. None I wanna get."

"You coulda fooled me," Cora said.

"What's up, kid?"

"Things are not going well. Becky's in a bind. Her investigator's on trial, which leaves her short one investigator."

"You couldn't just ask me for a favor?"

"Was I that obvious?"

"You sound like you're stoically joking in the face of death. You guys get a kick in the chops?"

Cora brought him up to date on the events in court.

"Could be worse," Crowley said. "What do you need from me?"

"Luke Haslett is the town drunk. It would be a miracle if he remembers anything at all. The way my luck's been running, he probably took a selfie in front of the burning puzzle."

"So whaddya want?"

"I need to know before we go to court. Chief Harper wouldn't tell me. He might tell you."

"He knows I'd just tell you."

"Exactly."

Crowley thought that over. "He's not going to be happy about it."

"I imagine not."

"Call you back."

"I'm on Becky Baldwin's cell phone. The number's —"

"I got it."

Cora handed the phone back to Becky. She put it down on the Country Kitchen bar and picked up her drink. "You think he'll get it?"

Cora shrugged. "There's a chance. Harper can't be happy about the situation. He'd love to tip me off as long as it wouldn't come back and bite him in the ass. Besides, it's a negative confirmation. It's not revealing any information, it's just confirming they don't have any."

Becky fiddled with her drink. "Look, it's none of my business —"

"I hate it when people say that. It means

they're about to ask something that's none of their business."

"That's what I said."

"Yeah. It's none of your business, but you're going to ask it anyway."

"I'm your lawyer."

"You're claiming it *is* your business?"

"You were seeing Roger Martindale."

"Allegedly."

"Oh, come on, Cora, it's just you and me. And I'm trying to think this thing out. Because you're not thinking as clearly as your average tree slug. So, if everything you're telling me is true —"

"Why would I lie to you?"

"I don't know why you do half of what you do, Cora. I know you're capable of anything."

"I'm not capable of killing Roger Martindale. Oh, all right, I *am* capable of it. But I wouldn't do it."

"If he was threatening your family?"

Cora told Becky what she thought of her hypothetical. Glasses on the shelf over the bar rattled.

The cell phone rang. Becky reached for it, but Cora beat her to it.

It was Crowley. "Bad news."

Cora's face fell. "What?"

"Harper wouldn't tell me anything."

"We expected that."

"Yes and no."

"Crowley, I'm not in the mood."

"I know. I told him I knew he couldn't tell me anything but I understood they picked up the town drunk, and there wasn't a snowball's chance in hell the guy knew anything. I figured he wouldn't get in trouble for telling me there was nothing new when there was nothing new."

"And?"

"He said he couldn't tell me that."

CHAPTER 48

"It's not so bad," Sherry said.

"What do you mean, it's not so bad? My best defense all along has been that Paula Martindale is a better suspect. If she's not a better suspect, I'm elected."

"But you don't know this guy can place her at the mall."

"Yes, we do. If he couldn't, Chief Harper would have said so."

"Yeah, but it's a negative confirmation. It doesn't say the guy's a solid witness, it says he can't be dismissed as knowing nothing at all. What little he does know will be shaky at best, almost certainly inconclusive. There's no way he gives the woman a rock-solid alibi."

"It's bad if he gives her anything at all. Becky doesn't have a lot of cards to play. It's bad news Ratface trumps her ace on the first trick."

"You've been playing too much bridge,"

Sherry said.

"Bridge," Cora said.

"What about it?"

"I met Paula Martindale playing bridge. If I were thinking straight, the word 'bridge' would conjure up an association, set me on the right track. I'd solve this thing in no time."

"You can't make an association if it isn't there."

"That never stopped me before. But today? Absolutely nothing. I mean, what, the old man didn't see Paula Martindale at the mall, he saw her crossing a bridge? Somehow, that doesn't help me."

"All right, what does?"

"I don't know." Cora glanced around. "You're awfully quiet, Aaron. Got anything to contribute?"

Aaron Grant was slumped in a chair, idly playing with one of Jennifer's dolls. He heaved a sigh. "I got nothing."

"Hey, take it easy," Cora said. "You're not the one going to jail."

"Sorry. I don't mean to be insensitive. It's just I can't bear to write about this."

"Oh, yeah?" Cora said. "Well, I got good news for you. *I didn't do it.* Ever since the case blew up, everyone's been moping around as if I'm guilty. I'm a foolish old woman who got herself into a mess. But I'm *innocent.* Even if I'm convicted of this crime, *I didn't do it."*

"Oh, give me a break," Sherry said. " 'Even if I'm convicted.' "

"Is it really so bad if they prove Paula Martindale didn't do it?" Aaron said. "I mean, just because she didn't do it doesn't mean you did."

"I'm sure Becky will advance that theory," Cora said. "And the odds of getting one person on the jury to believe it are probably only slightly worse than of winning the lottery."

"I'm glad Jennifer's in bed," Sherry said. "She's too young to deal with terminal depression."

"Better start teaching her," Cora said grimly.

CHAPTER 49

Everyone in Bakerhaven was in the courthouse.

With one exception.

"Your Honor," Henry Firth said, "before the jury is brought in, I have a matter to bring to your attention. Yesterday the name Luke Haslett came up in my direct examination of the witness Ken Jessup. Mr. Haslett was added to the prosecution's list of witnesses, and he was duly served with a subpoena to appear in court this morning."

"Why are you bringing this to my attention?"

"He's not here, Your Honor. Officer Dan Finley went to his house to get him, but he's not answering the door. I ask that Your Honor issue a bench warrant in his name, empowering Officer Finley to enter his house and bring him into court."

"So ordered. Is that all, Mr. Firth?"

"Yes, Your Honor."

"Bring in the jury."

As the jury was marched in and took their seats, Chief Harper reached for his cell phone and slipped out the door.

Dan Finley was glad to get the call. He was eager to get back to the courthouse, find out what was going on. He didn't like hanging out in the street, waiting for an old drunk.

Particularly Luke Haslett. Dan knew him well, had arrested him many times. Drunk and disorderly. Disturbing the peace. At least Dan would get some satisfaction out of hauling him into the courthouse instead of throwing him in a cell. Judge Hobbs had never had to deal with him until he sobered up. It would be fun to drop a fully intoxicated Luke Haslett in his lap.

Dan had never arrested Luke Haslett at his house. If he got home, Dan was happy to let him stay.

Dan pushed up the front window, reached through, and unlocked the front door. So much for security. He went in, and recoiled from the stench of stale whiskey.

Luke Haslett hadn't made it into bed. Dan wasn't surprised. In Luke's case, it was a wonder he'd managed to make it home. He'd gotten as far as the living room, where he'd collapsed in a heap on the floor. A pint of cheap bourbon lay empty beside him. Dan heaved a sigh. Hoped he wouldn't have to carry him.

Luke was lying facedown. Dan shook him, got no response. He rolled him over onto his back.

The body was stiff, the eyes open and glassy. A carving knife protruded from his chest.

There was no pulse, not that Dan needed to check.

Luke was clearly dead.

The hand that had been twisted underneath him clutched a paper.

It was a Sudoku.

						4		
4		3		7	6			
				2				
	9			3	5			1
				4	1	7		6
			4			8		
	2					6		9
	1	6	8					

CHAPTER 50

Henry Firth was beside himself. He paced the floor of the judge's chambers, too agitated to sit down. "Your Honor," he insisted, "the jury has to be told."

"The jury has to be told the witness isn't available," Becky said.

"The jury has to be told *why.*"

"The jury *will* be told why. Unfortunately, the man is dead."

"That's no explanation."

"That's a perfect explanation. No one expects to hear testimony from a dead man."

"Your Honor, the jury needs to know how he died."

"No, it doesn't," Becky said. "That has no bearing on the present case and would be wildly prejudicial to the defendant. If the jury is subjected to such prejudicial innuendo, it will be impossible to get a fair trial."

"What *innuendo*? The witness was *killed.*

That's a *fact.*"

"That's a *debatable* fact," Becky said. "You could call witnesses who would give the opinion the man was killed, and I would have the right to cross-examine. But that would be extremely prejudicial, and something the jury should not hear."

"It's prejudicial because your client killed the witness," Henry Firth said.

"See, Your Honor," Becky said. "That's the type of highly prejudicial, rash assumption the prosecutor wants to make in front of the jury. I don't think the situation could be clearer."

Judge Hobbs put up his hand. "The woman has a point. The jury needs to be told the man is dead. The cause of death is hardly relevant."

"It's *entirely* relevant, Your Honor. He was killed to prevent him from telling what he knows."

"And there's another rash assumption the prosecutor would like to make in front of the jury. There's no evidence of any such thing."

"Your Honor, I spoke to Luke Haslett yesterday after court. He was prepared to testify to nearly being run down in the mall parking lot, looking at the car that swerved around him, and seeing a woman in a car burning a paper."

"Paula Martindale?" Judge Hobbs asked.

"He didn't know Paula Martindale. I had hoped he would identify her in court."

"Was he shown a picture of Paula Martindale?"

"No, Your Honor."

"Why not?"

"Because then Ms. Baldwin would make a big deal about how he was identifying her from seeing her picture, not from seeing her in the parking lot."

"That I can believe," Judge Hobbs said. "I can see why it would be frustrating to lose this man as a witness. But that does not mean you can shortcut the rules of evidence."

"I'm not trying to shortcut anything. The jurors should know the truth. Not some la-di-da expurgated version of the truth because the real truth looks bad for the defendant."

"It only looks bad for the defendant if it's presented in the manner you intend to present it," Becky said. "Judge Hobbs should make the announcement and instruct the jury. We should keep out of it."

"That's not acceptable to the prosecution," Henry Firth said.

"You don't think I can be fair?" Judge

Hobbs said.

"Of course I do, Your Honor. But the rights of the people need to be protected. I don't intend to stipulate them away just because defense counsel isn't happy with the facts."

"No one's asking you to stipulate anything," Judge Hobbs said. "We are dealing with an unfortunate situation. I am attempting to resolve it expediently and legally. I will explain to the jury that Luke Haslett, the witness mentioned in Paula Martindale's and Ken Jessup's testimony and himself scheduled to be a witness, will not be able to appear because he has died. That they are to attach no weight to this incident, and that it should have no bearing on the testimony of any other witness."

"That's totally unsatisfactory, Your Honor," Henry Firth said.

"I beg your pardon?"

"No offense, Your Honor, but it doesn't explain anything."

"There's nothing to explain," Becky said. "The jury only know about the witness because they were in court listening to your questioning of Ken Jessup when Officer Finley burst in with the news that he was dead. Which, of course, he should not have done, but Chief Harper had his cell phone off because he was in court. So if you consider the police an extension of the legal department, this is a situation entirely of your own making. Were it not for that incident, there would be nothing to explain."

"Except the fact the witness didn't obey the summons in the first place."

"The jury wasn't in court when you made that announcement."

"I'm afraid she's right, Mr. Firth. You may not like it, but that's the way it's going to be."

Henry Firth exhaled angrily. "Very well, Your Honor. In that case, I ask for a continuance."

"That's unacceptable," Becky said.

"You object to a continuance?"

"Of course I do. Don't you see what he's doing? He's trying to circumvent your ruling. Since you won't let him tell the jury Luke Haslett was murdered, he wants to give them time to learn it from the media."

"But the jurors have been instructed not to discuss the case or listen to the media," Henry Firth said. "And I'm sure Judge Hobbs will reemphasize those instructions when granting the continuance."

"Jurors are human beings, Your Honor. There's no way they'll miss that coverage.

As the prosecutor well knows."

"You can't have a continuance," Judge Hobbs said. "I'll grant you an adjournment until ten o'clock tomorrow morning."

"That may not be sufficient, Your Honor. I've just lost a key witness."

"A witness you knew nothing about until yesterday," Becky pointed out. "Is your whole case based on one man?"

Judge Hobbs smiled at the prosecutor. "Got you again, Henry."

CHAPTER 51

If the jurors missed the coverage it wasn't Rick Reed's fault. "Cover-up murder!" Rick proclaimed in front of the police station. "Key prosecution witness Luke Haslett, silenced before he could testify! In a stunning turnaround, a crucial alibi witness, who could have established beyond a shadow of a doubt that Paula Martindale, previously accused of the murder of her husband, could not have done it, because she was nowhere near the scene of the crime when it took place, has been brutally slain before he could take the stand.

"So far, no one is accusing Cora Felton, the defendant in the case, of perpetrating this heinous act, yet she is clearly the one who benefits the most. Legal pundits speculate her only chance of acquittal is raising reasonable doubt that the wife, Paula Martindale, is more likely to have committed the crime. Take her out of the equation, and

Cora Felton has no chance. The testimony of Luke Haslett would have taken Paula Martindale out of the equation, and yet, at the last moment, another mathematician has stepped in and taken Luke Haslett out of the equation.

"Cora Felton's only defense is that she had no knowledge of what Luke Haslett would say on the stand. She and her attorney have both declined comment.

"One can only speculate what they must be thinking."

"I'm thinking, did he really say 'another mathematician stepped in'?" Cora said.

"The boy shouldn't play with metaphors," Becky said. "Well, you think there's a juror in town who managed to miss that?"

"If so, I'd nominate him for sainthood." Cora was doing her best Henry Firth impression, pacing Becky Baldwin's office very much in the way Henry Firth had paced Judge Hobbs's. "So, what do we do now?"

"You're asking me?"

"Well, you're the lawyer."

"Yes, and I will do everything legally in my power. I couldn't stop Henry Firth from getting an adjournment. Which is not as bad as a continuance but still long enough to poison the jury. So. Everyone thinks you killed Luke Haslett. Wanna convince me you didn't?"

Cora's mouth fell open. "You don't trust me?"

"I trust you. Now make me *believe* you. Go on. Convince me you didn't kill Luke Haslett."

"Are you serious?"

"Before we're done I'm going to have to convince a jury you didn't kill Luke Haslett. I'd at least like a line of argument. At the moment, I haven't got one. The only one who benefits from his death is you."

"As far as we know."

"And he had a Sudoku."

"Right. Because someone wanted to make it look like I did it. Though why I would kill him and leave a Sudoku as a calling card makes no sense at all."

"Did you solve the copy Chief Harper slipped you?"

"Of course I solved it. Here, look."

1	6	2	5	9	8	4	3	7
4	8	3	1	7	6	9	2	5
5	7	9	3	2	4	1	6	8
7	9	8	6	3	5	2	4	1
2	3	5	9	4	1	7	8	6
6	4	1	2	8	7	5	9	3
3	5	7	4	6	9	8	1	2
8	2	4	7	1	3	6	5	9
9	1	6	8	5	2	3	7	4

"See? They're just numbers," Cora said.

"Do they add up to anything?"

"They add up to the fact I do Sudoku. They add up to the fact someone killed Luke Haslett to frame me. Though I don't know why they need to. They seem to have me dead to rights anyway."

"Fine. Keep going."

"What do you mean, fine?"

"I need you to explain why Luke Haslett was killed," Becky said. "There's no good reason, so listing bad reasons is a start."

"Good Lord."

"Go ahead. Sell me. Why would the killer *need* to frame you?"

"I have no idea."

"So think it out. What does framing you accomplish?"

"Absolutely nothing. Except it draws attention away from the murder."

"The one you're being tried for?"

"Yeah, *that* murder. I didn't do that one, either, in case you're asking."

"I never said you did."

"You never said I *didn't.* Okay, why did the killer need to frame me? He didn't. So why did he do it? Maybe he didn't. If he *didn't* do it to frame me, then why did he do it? I have no idea, but take *that* as a premise. Luke Haslett could prove Paula Martindale's alibi, but he isn't needed. Why not? Because Paula has *another* way to prove her alibi? Not that we know of. Because he's not a good-enough witness to do it? More likely. He's a drunk and unreliable."

"Maybe there's something in his testimony that would *undermine* her alibi," Becky said.

"Perfect. But what could it be?"

"How about he remembers the whole incident but somehow manages to place it on a different date?"

"How could he possibly do that?" Cora said. "From what I understand, the man could barely remember his own name."

"So why do you silence a witness like that?"

"How the hell should I know?"

"We're not getting anywhere," Becky said.

"Yeah, because there's nowhere to get. We're speculating on the preposterous."

Becky shrugged. "That's what lawyers do."

Chapter 52

There was a change in the jury. They had been, if not sympathetic, at least neutral. Today their faces were hard. And as Judge Hobbs once again brought up the death of the witness Luke Haslett and instructed them not to speculate on what Mr. Haslett might have said, they all were looking straight at Cora Felton. A sure sign that they had made up their minds.

Henry Firth regarded them with satisfaction. His adjournment had done its job.

"Now then," Judge Hobbs said. "When we left off yesterday, the witness Ken Jessup was on the stand, and Mr. Firth was conducting his direct examination. Do you have any further questions, Mr. Firth?"

"Just a few, Your Honor."

"Proceed. Mr. Jessup, I remind you that you are still under oath."

"Mr. Jessup," Henry Firth said, "you testified to seeing Paula Martindale sitting alone in a car in the mall parking lot?"

"Yes, I did."

"You also testified to seeing Luke Haslett lurch in front of your car as you were driving out of the lot?"

"That was a separate incident."

"But you testified to it?"

"Yes."

"Mr. Jessup, would it surprise you to learn that Luke Haslett —"

"Objection!" Becky thundered. Jurors gawked in amazement to hear such a bellicose roar come out of such an attractive young woman.

"Sustained!" Judge Hobbs snapped. "Counsel, approach the bench!"

Becky and Henry Firth went up to confer with the judge.

"Mr. Firth," Judge Hobbs said with quiet intensity, "any attempt to circumvent the court's ruling by introducing anything Luke Haslett may or may not have told you outside of court while not under oath will be considered contempt of court and grounds for a mistrial. Do I make myself clear?"

"Yes, Your Honor."

"Step back."

The lawyers resumed their positions.

Henry Firth said, with rather bad grace,

"No further questions."

"Ms. Baldwin?" Judge Hobbs said.

Becky didn't even bother to stand. "No questions, Your Honor."

That produced a ripple in the court. Henry Firth nearly gagged.

"Very well," Judge Hobbs said. "The witness is excused. Call your next witness."

"Your Honor," Henry Firth said, "I find myself at a loss. The witness I intended to call, as you know, is not available, and I had expected counsel's cross-examination to take all morning. If I could have a brief recess?"

"The court was adjourned overnight so you could prepare, Mr. Firth."

"Yes, Your Honor. As I say, this took me by surprise. I need to line up a witness."

"Ten minutes, Mr. Firth. Not a minute more," Judge Hobbs said.

As court broke up, Paula Martindale pushed her way through the gate and grabbed Henry Firth. Her face was animated. She whispered something and pulled him out of earshot of the defense table.

"What the hell just happened?" Cora said.

"I don't know," Becky said, "but it can't be good."

CHAPTER 53

Henry Firth's manner had changed. When court recessed, he had seemed dejected and utterly at sea. When court reconvened, he seemed confident, eager, purposeful, almost gloating.

"Mr. Firth," Judge Hobbs said, "is your next witness ready?"

"Yes, Your Honor."

"Very well. Call your witness."

"Call Paula Martindale."

Becky Baldwin spread her arms. "Objection, Your Honor. Mr. Firth completed his direct examination of Paula Martindale and declined to rebut my cross-examination. Her testimony is done. He can't recall her on a whim. I submit that he has no purpose in mind, and he is recalling her merely because he is unprepared and has no witness ready."

"Is that true, Mr. Firth?"

"Not at all, Your Honor. New evidence

has come to light."

"Evidence you didn't have ten minutes ago when court recessed because you had no witness ready?"

"That's right."

"Very well. You may proceed."

Paula Martindale took the stand.

"Mrs. Martindale," Henry Firth said, "you testified to seeing Ken Jessup in the parking lot the night you burned the puzzle."

"Objected to as already asked and answered, leading and suggestive, and assuming facts not in evidence," Becky Baldwin said smoothly.

Judge Hobbs blinked. "Sidebar," he said ominously.

The lawyers approached the bench.

"You have *three* objections to counsel's question?" Judge Hobbs said.

"Your Honor, I object to this whole *line* of questioning. I know Your Honor has already ruled on that. I still maintain that Mr. Firth is stalling. The question has been already asked and answered, and I will object to anything that isn't new."

"The question was preliminary only, Your Honor," Henry Firth said.

"It would seem so, Ms. Baldwin."

"It's also leading and suggestive. Counsel is practically testifying for the witness. He delivered all the testimony, and the witness is simply supposed to say yes."

"I was merely trying to save time, summarizing things that, as you say, have already been asked and answered. Counsel is obviously not interested in saving time."

"And assuming facts not in evidence?" Judge Hobbs said.

"The prosecutor blithely refers to the parking lot where the witness burned the puzzle. That fact is very much not in evidence. Paula Martindale may have said she burned a puzzle, but we have only her word for it. That is not a fact in evidence. It is merely the unsubstantiated claim of an interested party."

"Oh, for God's sake," Henry Firth said.

Judge Hobbs put up his hand. "Hang on. Ms. Baldwin, I will very reluctantly sustain the objection on that grounds. Can you rephrase the question, Mr. Firth?"

"I have no objection to you referring to 'the occasion on which you *claim* you burned the puzzle,' " Becky said sweetly.

"I will withdraw the question," Henry Firth said. "Let's move on."

The lawyers resumed their positions.

"The question is withdrawn," Judge Hobbs said. "Mr. Firth?"

"Mrs. Martindale, on the occasion in the

parking lot when you say you burned the puzzle, did you recognize anyone *other* than Ken Jessup and Luke Haslett?"

"Yes, I did."

"And who would that be?"

"I don't know his name, but he's here in court. I saw him just before the recess and remembered he was one of the people I saw that night."

"Can you point him out to us?"

"Yes, of course. He's the young man sitting right over there with the other reporters."

Paula Martindale turned and pointed straight at Aaron Grant.

Chapter 54

"State your name."

"Aaron Grant."

"What is your relationship with the defendant?"

"I am married to her niece, Sherry Carter."

"Mr. Grant, were you in the parking lot of the Bakerhaven mall on the day that Roger Martindale was killed?"

"Yes, I was."

"Did you happen to see the witness, Paula Martindale, at the time?"

"Yes, I did."

"What was she doing?"

"Sitting in her car."

"Was she alone?"

"Yes, she was."

"Was she sitting in the driver's seat?"

"Yes."

"Was the window down or up?"

"The window was down."

"Did you see her do anything at the time?"

"Yes, I did."

"What did she do?"

"She burned something."

There was a reaction in the courtroom. Judge Hobbs banged the gavel.

Henry Firth smiled triumphantly. "What did she burn?"

"A piece of paper."

"Did you see what that piece of paper was?"

"I wasn't close enough to see."

"How big was it?"

"Not that big."

"The size of a sheet of typing paper?"

"Objection, Your Honor. Leading and suggestive."

"He's a hostile witness, Your Honor."

"He's shown no hostility so far. Try to avoid leading him."

"Mr. Grant, could you tell if the paper was *larger* than a standard sheet of typing paper?"

"No, I could not."

"Could you tell if it was smaller?"

"No."

"Could you see anything written or printed on it?"

"No, I could not."

"What color was the paper?"

"White."

"How did Paula Martindale burn the paper?"

"She held it out the window, lit it with a pocket lighter. She held it by one corner until it was almost entirely burned, then dropped it on the ground."

"What time was this?"

"I didn't look at my watch."

"Approximately what time was this?"

"I really couldn't say."

"Was it in the morning or afternoon?"

"It was in the afternoon."

"How did you come to be at the mall? Had you come from work?"

"That's right."

"What do you do, Mr. Grant?"

"I'm a reporter for the *Bakerhaven Gazette.*"

"You were at the paper before you went to the mall?"

"That's right."

"You went to the mall after work?"

"I'm a reporter, Mr. Firth. I went to the mall during work."

"Did you just run out to get something?"

"No."

"Were you on the job at the mall?"

"That's right."

"So when you say you were there during

work, you mean you were there in the course of your job?"

"That's right."

"Do you work regular hours, Mr. Grant?"

"Yes, I do."

"As a reporter, do you also work hours that are outside of your regular schedule?"

"Of course."

"When you say you were at work at the mall, it was not necessarily within nine-to-five business hours?"

"Objected to, Your Honor. Viciously leading and suggestive."

Judge Hobbs frowned. "In light of Mr. Grant's recent answers, I am now going to rule he is, if not hostile, at least a reluctant witness. I'm going to allow leading questions."

"When you say you were at the mall during work, that was not necessarily within nine-to-five business hours?"

"That's right."

"Why were you at the mall?"

"As the result of an anonymous news tip."

"What was that tip?"

"That high school students were getting high in the parking lot."

"Were you told what time this was happening?"

"Before dinner."

"People have dinner at different times, Mr. Grant. Were you told anything more specific than that?"

"No."

"Did you get the tip yourself?"

"Yes, I did."

"How did you get it?"

"It was a phone call."

"Who was on the phone?"

"I don't know. It was anonymous. A man just gave me the tip."

"And did you recognize his voice?"

"No, I did not."

"Did you go to the mall as soon as you got the tip?"

"No. I was working on a story. It had to be in before —" Aaron broke off.

"You were about to say a specific time, Mr. Grant. When did the story have to be in by?"

"Five o'clock."

"Did you make that deadline?"

"Yes, I did."

"You turned in the story and went to the mall?"

"That's right."

"I don't recall reading a story about students getting high at the mall. Did the tip pan out?"

"No, it did not."

"And how long did you wait at the mall to see if it might?"

"I don't remember."

"As long as an hour?"

"Probably."

"As long as two hours?"

"I don't remember."

"But it might have been two hours?"

"It's possible. I just don't remember."

"And how long after you got to the mall did you see Paula Martindale burn the puzzle?"

"Objection. Assuming facts not in evidence."

"How long before you saw Paula Martindale burn the *paper*?"

"I have no idea."

"Was it as soon as you got there?"

"No."

"Was it after you'd been waiting for some time?"

"I don't know how long."

"And how long after she burned the puzzle — excuse me, the paper — did you stay at the mall?"

"I don't remember."

"But at some time during the one to two hours you think you might have stayed in the mall parking lot, the witness Paula Martindale stuck her hand out the window of her car and burned the paper?"

"That's right."

"Thank you, Mr. Grant. No further questions."

"Ms. Baldwin?" Judge Hobbs said.

Becky stood up. "Your Honor, I'm not prepared for this witness. I was given no advance notice. I would ask for an adjournment."

"No objection," Henry Firth said. "I can understand why counsel might need time to regroup."

"Mr. Firth, such side comments are wholly inappropriate."

"Yes, Your Honor."

"Very well. Court is adjourned until tomorrow morning at ten o'clock."

CHAPTER 55

Aaron Grant was not having a good time of it. He, Sherry, and Cora were all crammed into Becky Baldwin's office, which somehow didn't seem big enough for the four of them.

"You couldn't tell me?" Sherry demanded.

"Sweetheart —"

"Don't 'sweetheart' me. Paula Martindale was on trial. Becky was defending her. Cora was trying to find anything to help her out. They desperately needed something to substantiate Paula's story. You had it, and you didn't speak up."

"You don't understand."

"*I* don't understand," Becky said. "You're a newsman. You had an exclusive and you kept it in your pocket."

"Scooping your own story is no scoop," Aaron said.

"You want a scoop?" Sherry said. "How about 'newsman divorced after trashing own family'?"

"Little long for a headline," Aaron said.

"You can joke about it?" Sherry said.

"Well, he's gotta do something," Cora said. "Look at the poor guy."

"You're sticking up for him?" Sherry said.

"Someone has to," Cora said.

"If I could just explain —"

"You can explain?" Becky said. "This I gotta hear."

"The thing is, I'm personally involved."

"You're involved with *Paula Martindale*?" Sherry said incredulously.

"Don't be silly. I'm involved with my family. I am, as Henry Firth pointed out, an interested party. Paula Martindale's on trial, Becky's defending her, Cora's doing her legwork. So what does she come up with? Her niece's husband. Who just happens to be in the right place at the right time to support the ridiculous alibi. How's that gonna look?"

"Better than nothing at all," Becky said.

"Yes, and if it had gotten that far, I would have come forward. But it didn't. Becky wasn't even presenting her case. Henry Firth was bumbling through his. If it developed that Paula Martindale *needed* my alibi, of course I would have given it. But as I recall, she never told her story until she fired Becky and turned against Cora. At which point you would have liked me to have jumped up and said, 'That's absolutely right, she has a rock-solid alibi, Cora must have done it.' "

"You could have told me," Sherry said.

"And what would you have done? You'd have insisted I tell Cora. Or you'd have told her. How helpful is that? Becky's building a case on the fact the prosecution can't prove she did it and Cora's presumed innocent. You want me to undermine that case? No, that case should play out, legally, in the court system. If the prosecutor finds me, of course I'm going to tell the truth, which I did. But I'm not screaming it from the housetops. Would you really want me to?"

"You should have told me from the beginning," Sherry said. "We're married. We don't keep secrets from each other."

"Welcome to *my* world," Cora said.

"That's not funny."

"No, it's not. But if you take the husband-wife dynamic out of the equation, there is this murder charge."

"Right," Becky said. "What difference does it make why Aaron didn't come forward before? He has now, and we have to deal with it."

"Yes, we do," Cora said. "If you girls would take a little walk?"

"What?" Sherry said.

"I'm the one going to jail. I'd like to talk to Aaron. Becky, why don't you take Sherry out for a spin. You've both had a bit of a shock. You've been betrayed by a man. It may be new to you, but it happens to be right in my wheelhouse. Take a little walk. Aaron and I will be right with you."

Reluctantly, Becky and Sherry left.

"You sent them out together?" Aaron said.

"You think that's a bad idea?"

"I can't think of much worse."

"Exactly. That's what I want to talk to you about."

"What?"

"I got rid of them so we can talk turkey. All this crap about you'd have come forward if you had to but it wouldn't look good because you're a member of the family, and Paula hadn't told her story yet, and all of the rest of the junk you thought up."

"It happens to be true."

"Yeah, it is. It's just not why you didn't come forward. Your ex-girlfriend was handling the case. You didn't want to be the knight in shining armor who comes charging in on his white steed to save the damsel in distress."

"Come on."

"Hey, you know how many times I've been

327

married? You know how many tall tales I've told to avoid telling the truth? This is a white lie, at the very worst. Hell, it's not even a lie, it's a sin of omission. You didn't want to set off an avoidable marital spat. The fact it morphed into you didn't want to send your wife's aunt up the river is entirely coincidental. So relax, take the body blows, tell them what they want to know. It can't hurt now, the worst is over."

Cora chucked Aaron on the arm. "Come on, let's go see if they killed each other."

CHAPTER 56

"So, you have a nice time with your boy-friend?"

"That's not funny," Becky said.

"Hey, I'm looking at a one-way ticket to the big house. You're faulting me on my sense of humor?"

"What's the matter, you got no confidence in your lawyer?"

"I've got confidence in her. Unfortunately, she's an attorney, not a magician."

"How can you say that, after I slept with Aaron Grant to try to get him to change his testimony?"

"That's more like it," Cora said. "If you can't laugh at your troubles, what's the use having troubles?"

Becky flung herself into her chair. "Yeah."

"I take it Aaron had nothing helpful to add."

"How could he? He's already done his worst. Nothing could make it any better. It can only make it worse."

"How, if he's already done his worst?"

"I'm sure he'll think of a way." Becky took a breath. "Look, we've got to do some serious reevaluating. By all rights Paula Martindale killed Roger. He's her husband, she's a bitch, she's covered in blood, holding the knife. She practically had the word 'guilty' tattooed on her forehead. Lo and behold, thanks to Aaron Grant, of all people, she couldn't possibly have done it."

"Maybe Barney blew the time of death."

"Maybe, but try to prove it. I can cross-examine till I'm blue in the face, trying to stretch the parameters of the time he was killed, but all I'm doing is stretching the bounds of reason. When you're relying on reasonable doubt, reason is one thing you don't want to stretch."

"So what do we do now?" Cora said.

"I thought loopy bright ideas were your business."

"I'm out of bright ideas."

"How about loopy dumb ones?"

"Now you're talking." Cora settled back in her chair. "Okay, nothing sane works. We gotta try something *in*sane. How about Luke Haslett?"

"What about him?"

"Let's drag him into the case."

Becky stared at her. "Cora, I just used every trick in the book to keep him *out* of the case."

"Right. That's why it's a loopy *bad* idea."

"It's not just bad. It's suicidal. Are you forgetting you're the only one with a motive to kill Luke Haslett?"

"Yeah, but I'm not being tried for that."

"Cora."

"Look, I didn't bring Luke Haslett into the case, she did, with all the talk about a drunk stumbling in front of the car. Frankly, I didn't believe it. I thought Luke Haslett was a witness she trumped up to bolster her story. Which made sense as long as she was guilty. If she's innocent, I'm wrong. And Luke Haslett was a real witness all along."

"He had to be a real witness. Ken Jessup saw him."

"Unless Ken Jessup was a phony witness, too."

"He hates Paula Martindale."

"Well, don't give him too much credit. So do I."

"Cora, this isn't helping. You said you wanted to bring Luke Haslett into this."

"Yeah."

"Why?"

"Well, Ratface won't expect it. It'll be worth it just to see the look on his face."

"What's the practical value in terms of this case?"

"I have no idea."

"I'm glad we had this little talk."

Cora yawned and stretched. "I'll tell you what I don't understand," she said. "And, yes, I know that yawning is a defense mechanism to mask fear. I don't understand why she brought Luke Haslett into this in the first place."

"She needed a witness."

"He's a terrible witness. He's a hopeless drunk whose memory is going to be faulty at best. Whose testimony could probably be bought with a pint of cheap rum. His credibility is virtually non-existent."

"He was there. He was a disheveled drunk so he stood out. One recognizable face in a vast sea of middle-class mediocrity."

"Whoa!" Cora said. "Listen to Little Miss Law Degree. Throw a dose of adversity in her face and real, true feelings come out."

"And it's not like she named him as her witness. She named Ken Jessup. Luke Haslett was an afterthought. She didn't even know his name. If Ken Jessup hadn't identified him, he might have escaped unnoticed."

"And what's with that?" Cora said. "Ken Jessup is a terrible witness, too. He's wildly prejudiced and isn't going to do anything to

332

help her. Look how elusive he was about the time all this happened. He wouldn't even put it on the same *day.*"

"She noticed him because he was a friend of her husband," Becky said. "She's upset, all she's thinking about is her husband. Nothing else is going to ring a bell. She noticed him in particular because she almost got out of her car to talk to him before realizing that was a bad idea. She named him because he may be wildly prejudiced, but she doesn't think he'd have the guts to lie under oath."

"I could buy all that except for one thing," Cora said.

"What's that?"

"Aaron Grant. He's a wonderful witness. He saw everything, and he's totally unbiased. Well, at least until I'm the defendant. Then he's out to get me."

"Cora."

"She tells you she burned the puzzle at the mall. She knows you don't believe her, or at least are very skeptical, and you're not going to let her say it on the stand. That is the time to trot out Aaron Grant. Instead of a morose, depressed lawyer fighting for every foothold, suddenly, you're megabitch attorney, striding into court and kicking the prosecutor's ass."

"She didn't remember Aaron Grant."

"Until court broke for recess today? Give me a break."

"She saw him in court."

"Yeah. Up front in the press row. Where he's been sitting every day since the beginning of *her* trial. She just sees him now?"

"It happens. She just happened to glance over."

"Right. On the very day her witness is dead and her alibi falls apart. I don't buy it. She had him in her hip pocket. He was her trump card, she was just waiting to play it. Meanwhile, she's putzing around with her other two witnesses."

"If you say so."

"I do. And that's what I can't figure. Aaron Grant is gold. If you have him, why do you need them at all?"

"I have no idea. Maybe it will come out on the stand."

"What do you mean?"

"When I question Aaron Grant."

Cora sighed, shook her head. "Don't."

"Don't what?"

"Question Aaron Grant. He's in enough trouble at home as it is. Let him go."

Becky stared at her. "Cora, Aaron just gave Paula Martindale her alibi. If that stands up, I don't know if I can save you."

"Well, don't browbeat it out of Aaron Grant."

"You're kidding, right?"

"No."

"You want me to go easy on him?"

"I want you to let him go."

"What do you mean?"

"Don't question him at all."

"I can't let his testimony stand uncontested."

"You think he's lying?"

"No, but —"

"There you are. He's telling the truth. I don't know how it happened, but it happened. Nothing's gonna make it any better."

Cora shook her head. "Let him go."

CHAPTER 57

Dinner that night was strained at best. Only Jennifer was oblivious to the tension in the air. She had had a wonderful day in preschool, painting a picture of what was either a green and yellow backhoe or a rather grotesque frog. It was almost dry when she proudly bore it home. Sherry was lucky to keep it off the seat of the car.

The meal was microwave frozen pasta. Sherry hadn't been in the mood to cook, and no one could blame her. The tortellini weren't bad but lacked that home-style touch.

"I think you two should get away for a little vacation," Cora said.

Sherry's mouth fell open. "Are you kidding me?"

"No. I thought about kidding you; it didn't seem like a good time."

"Cora —" Aaron said.

"Oh, please don't apologize again," Cora

said. "I got myself into this mess, and I'll get myself out of it. Pass the grated cheese."

The Parmesan was also store-bought rather than shaved Reggiano. Cora shook some out on the tortellini, considered the result, shook out a little more. "Why don't you rent a house on the beach and take off for a week. I'm sure Jennifer would love the seashore."

"We're not going to go off and leave you," Sherry said.

"Oh, *please* go off and leave me," Cora said. "It's like living in one of those depressing subtitled movies where you keep praying the projector will break down. I'm a very poor marriage counselor, even under the best of circumstances when I'm not on trial for murder."

"You're not helping," Aaron said.

"Oh, you're blaming her?" Sherry said.

"Maybe you shouldn't come to court tomorrow," Aaron said.

"And miss your old girlfriend tearing you to bits?" Sherry said. "Not a chance."

"Becky wouldn't do that," Cora said.

"She wouldn't do that to Aaron? Maybe you should get another lawyer."

"I should get another plate of pasta," Cora said.

"Getting fat will just make you depressed,"

Sherry said.

"Oh? What will cheer me up?"

"Actually, you're in an awfully good mood," Aaron said. "What gives?"

"I'm punchy. After a while you get punchy."

"See what you've done?" Sherry said.

"Aw, hell," Cora said. Instead of getting more pasta, she put her plate in the sink and clomped down the hall to her office.

The computer was on. She had mail. Maybe it was something that would help . . . Only if she were embarrassed in the locker room. Cora deleted the message, scanned the recently arrived. Sherry often picked up Cora's email to see if there were Puzzle Lady queries she needed to answer, so just because messages were marked "read" didn't mean Cora had seen them. Today she had, and they were all about the trial. Sympathy and support was running neck and neck with how-could-you-do-such-a-thing?

Cora went across the hall, flopped down on her bed, flipped on the TV.

Rick Reed was holding forth. The last thing in the world she wanted to hear. She put the TV on Mute.

It was strange. Rick Reed looked smarter when you couldn't hear him. A smart Rick

Reed was more than she could bear. Cora zapped the sound back on.

". . . a tough job," Rick Reed said. "Becky Baldwin has to find some way to cross-examine Aaron Grant that doesn't crucify her client. It seems an impossible task. The smart move would be to get Aaron Grant off the stand before he does any more harm. In the opinion of this reporter, she probably shouldn't cross-examine at all."

Cora zapped the TV to Mute again.

Waves of depression swept over her. Here she was, facing a murder conviction, and the best she could come up with was the wisdom of Rick Reed.

And yet, there was nothing else to do. Aaron Grant couldn't help her. Every question Becky asked would only sink her more. It would cost Cora her liberty and Sherry her marriage.

Was it worth it, not to take the advice of Rick Reed?

Henry Firth's face filled the screen. Cora could practically see his ratty nose twitching, smelling the victory. She zapped the sound on again.

"Mr. Firth," Rick Reed said, "if you get a conviction in the Roger Martindale case, would you turn around and try Cora Felton for the murder of Luke Haslett?"

The prosecutor smiled, put up his hand. "One thing at a time, Rick. It is really premature to start talking about a murder conviction," he said magnanimously, "when the defense has not yet begun to put on its case."

"What defense could they possibly have?"

"I can't speak for the defense. I can only speak for the prosecution."

"The prosecution must be feeling pretty good right about now."

"Two men were killed, Rick. I don't feel good about that. But I am confident of a conviction."

"That was Henry Firth, speaking for the prosecution in the trial of Cora Felton for the murder of Roger Martindale. The defense declined comment. Rick Reed, Channel Eight News."

Cora muted Rick Reed again, sank into a deeper depression. She hadn't considered being tried for the murder of Luke Haslett. That was, however, a very real possibility. She barely knew the details of the crime. She'd have to do some rather thorough investigating, and it might be difficult if she was incarcerated.

Her spiral of despair was twisting rapidly down. Ken Jessup, Luke Haslett, Aaron Grant, oblivion. Not a nice progression.

Think, you moron, she told herself.
What the hell can you possibly do?

CHAPTER 58

Becky Baldwin muted Rick Reed in the same place Cora had. This was not a co-incidence. Muting Rick Reed was one of Becky Baldwin's favorite occupations.

Becky got up off the couch, went to see what was in the fridge. It was not a long trip. Becky's apartment, on the top floor of Mrs. Taggart's house, was not extensive. It resembled an artist's garret more than a lawyer's apartment. The eaves made it impossible to stand upright, except in the center of the room, which was long and nar-row and divided up like a railroad flat without partitions. Becky intended to move out as soon as her practice became success-ful.

She'd lived there for years.

The fridge was not well stocked. She found a few leaves left from a head of romaine lettuce, half a red pepper, a few radishes, and a cucumber. That would do for a salad. There was still a little left of the balsamic vinaigrette she'd made the day before. Becky took out a bowl, prepared to toss the salad. She had to keep up her strength without putting on weight. It was depressing enough barely getting by. She couldn't bear the thought of fat and forty. Not that she was anywhere near forty, but that was something she could do nothing about. Fat, she could. Becky still looked like she'd be comfortable on a catwalk.

There was some leftover chicken. Becky cut off a couple of slices, put them on a plate with the salad, poured herself a glass of wine, and went back to eat in front of the TV.

She clicked through the schedule, scanned the evening's programming. There was a lawyer show. Becky wasn't up for a lawyer show. A stupid sitcom would do the trick. The ones offered were too stupid. She'd tried them before. Couldn't stomach them, either.

Becky sighed. It was frustrating as hell. Aaron Grant gets on the witness stand, decimates her client, and she can't do anything about it. Because her client forbade her. As if she were a small child.

Should she ignore the wishes of her client? Sure, if she wanted to be disbarred.

343

Her client was Cora Felton. Cora was capable of standing up in court and saying, "I told you not to do that." It would be contempt of court, but that wouldn't stop Cora. She was facing a murder count. Would a contempt of court citation faze her?

So Becky couldn't cross-examine Aaron, Henry Firth would go on all morning using Aaron, and by extension, Becky and Cora, as a punching bag. And she'd just have to sit there and take it.

Becky nibbled on a piece of lettuce. Tried to think of a way to change Cora's mind. That wasn't a very likely prospect. She'd be better off attacking the follow-up witness, which there would have to be. Just because Paula Martindale didn't kill her husband didn't mean Cora Felton did. Though it surely would in the minds of the jurors. And Henry Firth would drive the point home before Becky could raise reasonable doubt.

What reasonable doubt? Becky was beginning to reasonably doubt her own client. So how could she keep the jury from doing it?

That, Becky realized, was going to take a miracle.

She was sunk if she couldn't cross-examine Aaron Grant.

The phone rang.

Becky scooped it up. Wondered what fresh

hell this might be.

"Becky, it's Cora. Remember what I said about not cross-examining Aaron Grant?"

"I know. I won't do it."

"Forget it. Let 'er rip."

Chapter 59

"Mr. Grant," Becky said, "you were in court for the testimony of Paula Martindale, were you not?"

"Yes, I was."

"And you heard her testify about seeing you in the mall parking lot?"

"Yes, I did."

"And was her testimony accurate? With regard to seeing you on that occasion?"

"Yes, it was."

"Entirely accurate?"

"As far as I can recall."

"You saw her sitting in the car?"

"Yes, I did."

"You saw her burn something?"

"I saw her burn a paper."

"She burned a white sheet of paper?"

"That's right."

"But you couldn't see what was written on it?"

"No, I couldn't."

"And when she burned the paper — was that the only time you saw her at the mall?"

Aaron frowned. "I don't understand the question."

"You stated that you went to the mall as a result of a tip, and you waited in the parking lot for as much as one to two hours. Is that right?"

"Yes, it is."

"During that time, was the only time you saw Paula Martindale when she burned the paper?"

"No, it was not."

"You saw her sitting there before she burned the paper?"

"Yes, I did."

"And you saw her sitting there after she burned the paper?"

"Yes, I did."

"Was she there when you got there?"

"No, she arrived shortly thereafter."

"How long after that did she burn the paper?"

"I don't recall."

"Was it right away?"

"No."

"It was after some time?"

"Yes."

"As much as an hour?"

"No."

"Half an hour?"

"Possibly. I'm not sure."

"Twenty minutes?"

"That's more likely. I really couldn't say."

"And did she stay in the parking lot after she burned the paper?"

"Yes, she did."

"Did she stay long?"

" 'Long' is a relative term."

"Well, you say. How long did she stay in the parking lot?"

"I really can't remember."

"As long as half an hour?"

"Possibly."

"It might have been?"

"It might."

"So you would put her at the mall for approximately one hour encompassing the time her husband was killed."

Aaron took a breath. "That's right."

"Interesting," Becky said. "Let me ask you this. During that sixty-some minutes that you saw the defendant, did you see the witness Luke Haslett?"

"I don't recall seeing Luke Haslett."

"You don't?"

"No."

"Directing your attention to the time Paula Martindale burned the paper, did you see Luke Haslett walking by her car and nearly getting run over?"

"No, I did not."

"And did you see the witness Ken Jessup?"

"I don't recall seeing him."

"The witness Ken Jessup said that he walked by the car and shortly thereafter drove by it, nearly running over Luke Haslett. Did you see that?"

"No, I didn't."

"To the best of your recollection, when Paula Martindale burned the piece of paper, was there anyone else around?"

"No."

"Are you sure?"

"I had parked my car so I had a clear, unobstructed view of the front of Walmart. I also had a clear, unobstructed view of Paula Martindale's car, which was right in my sight line."

"Was there anything else in your sight line when you saw her burn the paper?"

"No."

"Are you sure?"

"I saw it clearly."

"Thank you, Mr. Grant. No further questions."

"Any redirect, Mr. Firth?"

"No, Your Honor."

"Very well, the witness is excused. Call your next witness."

Cora Felton stood up. "Before he does, Your Honor, I wonder if we could have a brief recess. I'd like to talk plea bargain."

There was a stunned silence in the courtroom.

Judge Hobbs's mouth fell open. He recovered, banged the gavel. "Miss Felton, you are out of order. Counselor, could you please control your client!"

"I can *try,* Your Honor."

There was a ripple of amusement in the courtroom.

"Ms. Baldwin, this is not a laughing matter. Your client has just made a particularly inappropriate remark in open court in the presence of the jury.

"Miss Felton, you are risking a contempt of court citation."

Cora shrugged. "How much trouble can I be in, Your Honor? I'm already on trial for murder. Contempt of court is a parking ticket."

"It's a one-thousand-dollar parking ticket, and you just earned it. Counselor, control your client."

"Yes, Your Honor. Sit down, Cora."

"Court is in recess for half an hour. Rein in your client, Ms. Baldwin, or the rest of this trial will take place in her absence."

With that, Judge Hobbs strode from the courtroom.

CHAPTER 60

Henry Firth had the smug assurance of a winner. "I'm genuinely sorry you're guilty," he said, "but I'm glad you decided to plea-bargain. I think in light of your cooperation, I can probably persuade Judge Hobbs to make that contempt citation go away."

"That's nice of you, Henry," Cora said.

Becky let out a relieved sigh. She'd been afraid Cora was going to call him Ratface.

"So, Becky, what's your offer?"

"So familiar, Henry," Cora said. "People will think you two are dating."

Becky turned to Cora. "If you spread any more rumors about me . . ."

"Spread? What do you mean, spread? It's just the three of us here."

"Don't play innocent with me. I know what you're capable of."

"Becky, this is neither the time nor the place."

"Has that ever stopped you before?"

"Must you make a scene in front of Henry Firth?"

"Must *I* make a scene?" Becky said. "You know, the last time you started rumors about me having an affair with Barney Nathan, it was to cover up the fact you were having an affair with Barney Nathan. Can I assume you're having an affair with Henry Firth?"

"Becky. Henry Firth is married."

"So was Barney Nathan."

"He still is. I'm not necessarily a deal breaker."

Henry Firth's eyes were getting wider and wider. He could sense his plea bargain slipping away. "Ladies, ladies . . . Do you want to plea-bargain or not?"

"My client does," Becky said. "Frankly, I don't agree, but she's calling the shots."

"So what's your offer?"

"All right," Cora said. "Here's the deal. Becky doesn't want to give you anything, but *she's* not the one with the thousand-dollar fine. If you could make that go away, I would be very grateful."

"It can probably be arranged."

" 'Probably' is not the type of word you want to hear in a plea bargain."

"If we reach an agreement, you won't have to pay."

"That's more like it. Okay, drop the murder charge and I'll plead guilty to trespassing."

Henry Firth's mouth fell open. He stared at her incredulously. "What?"

"Yeah," Cora said. "Like I say, Becky doesn't want to give you anything, but I'm just a nice girl. See, here's how I figure. Chief Harper is the chief of police, but I'm just an ordinary citizen. When we went out to Paula Martindale's house, I pushed my way in ahead of him. Which I had no right to do. That, I believe, would technically make me guilty of trespassing, and if you want to press the issue, I'm willing to concede the charge."

"The charge is murder," Henry Firth said. "I'm willing to listen to a charge of second-degree, or perhaps even manslaughter, but I am not interested in these minor crimes."

"That's too bad," Cora said. "I'm not guilty of anything more serious."

"I might have known this was just one of your charades," the prosecutor said angrily.

"Henry, Henry, calm down," Cora said. "We're friends. We're practically family. If I can't help you one way, I'll help you another. Tell him, Becky."

"You can put Cora on the stand," Becky said.

"What?"

"Call her as *your* witness. Get her declared hostile. Ask her leading questions."

"Are you serious?"

"Absolutely."

"I didn't expect you to put her on the stand at all. Are you saying you'd let me cross-examine her before you even present her case?"

"That's right."

Henry Firth looked at Cora suspiciously. "Why?"

CHAPTER 61

When court reconvened, Henry Firth stood up and addressed the judge. "Your Honor, in view of the fact Cora Felton has decided to cooperate with the prosecution, I would ask that her contempt citation be vacated and her fine rescinded."

"Do I understand you have reached an agreement with the defendant's attorney with regard to reducing the charges?"

"That is yet to be determined. But we are agreed in principle and would like to proceed."

Judge Hobbs blinked. "You have reached a plea-bargain agreement but you wish to proceed with the trial?"

"That's right."

"I don't understand."

"The defense has made certain concessions that will allow the trial to reach a speedy conclusion. In view of her cooperation, I would hope that Your Honor would vacate the citation."

Cora Felton cleared her throat.

"The defendant would appear to be on the verge of another citation," Judge Hobbs said dryly.

"Not at all, Your Honor," Becky Baldwin said. "My client is reacting to the word 'hope.' My client is not about to concede her rights based on the prosecutor's wishes, no matter how ardent. She is willing to co-operate with everyone, but she doesn't want this trial to cost her any more than it already has. It will take her several years to pay off my fee alone."

Cora gagged, shuddered, glared daggers at her attorney.

"That is hardly the concern of the court," Judge Hobbs said.

"No, but the administration of justice is," Henry Firth said. "In the interest of justice, I would like to wipe the slate clean and start again."

"Very well. Miss Felton, I will withdraw your fine. But be warned: I could reinstate it at any time. I could even double it."

"Yes, Your Honor," Cora said.

Judge Hobbs took a breath. "Please speak through your attorney."

"She understands, Your Honor," Becky said.

"Very well. Bring in the jury and call your next witness."

When the jurors had filed in and been seated, Henry Firth said, "Your Honor, I call Cora Felton."

Whatever Judge Hobbs had been expecting, it was not that. He froze with his mouth open. "I beg your pardon? Did you say Cora Felton?"

"Yes, Your Honor."

"Miss Felton. Do you realize you are under no obligation to testify?"

"She does, Your Honor," Becky said.

"This is most irregular," Judge Hobbs said. Then, realizing the jurors were in the room, "Very well. Miss Felton will take the stand."

Cora was sworn in and sat on the witness stand.

"Miss Felton," Judge Hobbs said, "you understand that you have the right to refuse to answer any question that you feel might tend to incriminate you?"

"Am I allowed to answer that, Your Honor?"

"I want you to."

"Yes, I understand that. I have a very capable attorney to protect my rights."

"And I'm sure she appreciates the recommendation, though this is not the time to be making it. You realize you are waiving your rights not to be called as a witness against yourself?"

"Yes, Your Honor."

"Very well. Proceed, Mr. Firth."

"Your name is Cora Felton?"

"That's right."

"You are the defendant in this action?"

"I am."

"You're a hostile witness?"

"Well, I'm not happy about it."

"You're giving your testimony reluctantly?"

"I'm in *court* reluctantly. You think I like being put on trial?"

"Your Honor, I would ask that you consider Miss Felton a hostile witness."

"That's a strange request, Mr. Firth. She doesn't have to be on the stand at all."

"I would like to ask leading questions."

"You may ask them. If Ms. Baldwin objects, her objection will be sustained."

"Thank you, Your Honor. Miss Felton, were you having an affair with the decedent, Roger Martindale?"

"Sure."

A loud murmur greeted that announcement.

"I beg your pardon," Henry Firth said. "Did you say you *were* having an affair?"

"Sure, I was. I mean, come on, look at his wife. The poor guy needed some amusement."

"Did you see him at the Fifty-seventh Street hotel?"

"That's right."

"Did you ever see his wife there?"

"Yeah. The last time I went. I saw her staking out the lobby. So I didn't go in. I called Roger, told him all bets were off, and to get the hell out of there."

"Did you see him again after that?"

"No, I did not."

"How about the twenty-four hours before his death when he was declared a missing person: Did you see him then?"

"No. The first I knew he was missing was when Chief Harper called me and asked me to intercede with Paula Martindale. He said he couldn't act on the complaint because it hadn't been twenty-four hours, but he'd appreciate it if I'd look into it."

"Which you did?"

"I talked to the wife. Who presented me with a crossword. Which Chief Harper knew she had. I still haven't forgiven him for that."

"This is not the puzzle Paula Martindale burned at the mall?"

"No. This is another puzzle entirely. A puzzle Paula Martindale got the day before her husband was killed. It said, 'Let this be a stop sign, don't touch what's mine.' "

"Did the crossword have any bearing on the case?"

"It confused it."

"How?"

"It implied he was having an affair. And it was, in fact, a crossword puzzle. Which was naturally attributed to me." Cora cocked her head. "I would imagine the only reason you haven't introduced it in this case is the killer neglected to upload it onto my computer. Which was a real oversight. If I'd made up the puzzles, both of them should be there."

"Where were you at the time of the murder?"

Cora made a face. "Unfortunately, my alibi is not as good as Paula Martindale's. I was out at the old Dairy Queen."

"Was anyone else out there?"

"It's been closed for years. Before I moved to town."

"What were you doing there?"

"I got a phone call, telling me to go."

"From whom?"

"I don't know. It was a man's voice. It sounded disguised. Said if I wanted to see Roger Martindale again, I should park behind the Dairy Queen and I would be contacted."

"Which you did?"

"It was tricky. I'd just had a phone call from Chief Harper, telling me Roger Martindale had been put on the missing persons list and asking me to come to the station."

"What did you tell him?"

"I told him I'd be right there."

"But you didn't go?"

"No. I went to the Dairy Queen first. I hung out as long as I dared. When no one showed up, I went to the police station to meet the chief."

"Did you tell anyone about this phone call asking you to go to the Dairy Queen?"

"No, I didn't."

"Including your lawyer?"

Cora shook her head. "I figured it would muddy the waters. I had no idea why I'd gotten the call. But it wasn't relevant to Paula Martindale's defense. And I didn't want to bring it up."

"Why not?"

"I was having an affair with Roger Martindale. I had hoped it wouldn't come out. When it did, Paula fired Becky, and I became the defendant. It certainly didn't seem a good thing to mention then."

"But you're mentioning it now."

"Well, I saw a chance to get out of a

thousand-dollar fine."

"Surely that's not the only reason."

"I happen to be innocent, and the only way to prove it is telling the truth."

"Isn't that always the case?"

"How can you say that? You're a prosecutor."

The remark drew a laugh. Judge Hobbs banged the gavel. "Miss Felton, try to confine yourself to answering the questions, not sparring with the prosecutor."

"Yes, Your Honor."

"How long did you wait at the Dairy Queen?"

"Not long. Then I hung it up and went to meet the chief. We went out to the decedent's house."

"What happened when you got there?"

"The door was open. I pushed my way in. Chief Harper wouldn't have approved, but I didn't wait for him. I was upset, and I went right in."

"What did you find?"

"Paula Martindale came out of the living room covered with blood, holding a knife. Chief Harper ordered her to drop it. When she didn't comply, he pulled his gun."

"What happened then?"

"She still didn't drop it. I grabbed her arm and twisted. That did the trick. She dropped the knife. I restrained her, and Chief Harper pushed by us into the living room."

"Did you see for yourself?"

"Yes, I did. I wrestled Paula Martindale to the door, looked in. Her husband was dead on the floor. Blood was everywhere."

"What did you do then?"

"I was stunned. I thought it was my fault. Paula Martindale had found out her husband was having an affair, flipped out, and killed him. It was a shock to find out she couldn't have done it."

"Just a minute. You are stating, on the witness stand, under oath, that in your opinion Paula Martindale did not do it?"

"Of course she didn't."

"How do you know?"

"Aaron Grant wouldn't lie. He can place her at the mall at the time of the murder."

"You're willing to concede that? Even though it might be your best defense?"

"My best defense is the truth. And that's the truth. Paula Martindale didn't do it."

"And you claim you didn't, either?"

"Of course not."

"You can see how it would look like you did? Chief Harper calls you, tells you Roger Martindale is on his way home. Instead of going to meet Chief Harper, you go somewhere else, right after phone records prove you got a call from Roger Martindale's cell. You show up late for your meeting with the chief, you accompany him to Paula Martindale's house, and at the first opportunity you manage to smear yourself with blood, just in case Chief Harper should notice you have blood on your clothes."

"My, I must be very clever. But this always was a particularly clever crime."

"In what way?"

"Look at the way I was framed. The killer doesn't just frame me, the killer frames me so it doesn't look like a frame. How does the killer do that? By leaving the crossword puzzle, which would be attributed to me if it weren't so incredibly stupid to think I would leave one. The killer gets around that by making it look initially like someone else committed the crime. But a bluff is only good if you carry it through. The killer carried it through to the point of having Paula Martindale arrested and tried for the murder. It's only after she's in court that the devastating evidence against me comes out. When it does, you take the puzzle at face value, because now it's a stupid frame-up once removed.

"Leaving a Sudoku with Luke Haslett is really pushing it. But that's okay, because it's the secondary murder, which the judge most likely won't let come into the trial anyway. And by the time I'm on trial for killing him, the prosecutor will have some sort of conviction in this case, so when he tries that case I'll be presumed guilty.

"I got to admit, it's a pretty clever plan, making it look so bad for Paula Martindale she can't help but be arrested for it. Covered in blood, holding a knife? Come on. That's a really dangerous step to take, and I'm sure the killer wouldn't have done it if Paula didn't have such a perfect alibi.

"But that was carefully planned, too."

"How?"

"Simple. Ken Jessup, who hates her guts, sees her sitting in her car. Naturally, he wouldn't want to admit it, but being a Milquetoast, he'd be too cowardly to lie about it. He places her at the mall, but at no particular time.

"Luke Haslett nails it. He saw her burn the puzzle."

"I beg your pardon?" Henry Firth said. "You said, 'the puzzle'?"

"That's right."

"Your attorney objected to the word 'puzzle' as assuming facts not in evidence. We've been referring to it as 'the paper.' "

"Yeah, I know. But everyone in this court-room knows it was a puzzle. Let's call it 'the puzzle.' He saw Paula Martindale burn the puzzle. *And* he almost got run over by Ken Jessup. Tying those two things together puts Paula Martindale in the parking lot at the time of the crime. Voilà, she could not do it.

"My first thought was that story was false, both witnesses were phony, somehow the testimony was trumped up to make it look like Paula Martindale was at the mall, when in actuality she was at home killing her husband. But that was dead wrong. There was another witness, Aaron Grant, who saw her there at the exact time of the crime, burning the puzzle, just like Luke Haslett said. Suddenly, instead of two iffy witnesses who could be lying or mistaken, Paula has three rock-solid alibi witnesses, absolutely conclusive proof that she could not have done it."

"Are you saying she did it anyway?"

"Of course not. Aaron Grant wouldn't lie. And he wouldn't be mistaken, either. He's a newsman. He gets things right. If he says she was at the mall, she was at the mall. Which pretty much settled things.

"Only one thing bothered me. Well, actually, several things — I *was* about to go down for a murder rap. I mean, one thing about her alibi. And that was Aaron Grant.

He was the perfect witness. No one could possibly doubt him. Paula Martindale was off the hook.

"What bothered me was Ken Jessup and Luke Haslett. They were terrible witnesses. If she had Aaron Grant, why did she need them?"

"She didn't know she had Aaron Grant," Henry Firth pointed out. "She just saw him in court."

"Yeah, and if you believe that, I'd like to get you at the poker table. She knew about him all along. In which case, why did she need Ken Jessup and Luke Haslett to alibi her?

"It took me a while to realize that they weren't."

Henry Firth frowned. "What?"

"They weren't alibiing her. *She* was alibiing *them.* So that everyone would be convinced that Ken Jessup was at the mall watching her in the parking lot instead of at her house killing her husband."

The courtroom burst into a babble of voices.

Judge Hobbs banged the gavel. "Order! Order! Bailiff, is the witness Ken Jessup in court?"

"He got up and went out a few minutes ago, Your Honor."

Chief Harper headed for the door as the court went wild.

CHAPTER 62

"Bombshells in Bakerhaven!" Rick Reed declared from the steps of the county courthouse. "In one stunning twist after another, the trial of Puzzle Lady Cora Felton for the murder of Roger Martindale came to an unexpected conclusion as crusading prosecutor Henry Firth dismissed all charges against Miss Felton. In an unprecedented move, at least one this courtroom journalist has never seen before, the defendant dazzlingly doubled as a prosecution witness and laid out the plans of the plot."

Sherry Carter, watching from the crowd, whispered, "Alliteration-happy, isn't he?"

"*That's* what bothers you?" Aaron Grant said. "He just described himself as a courtroom journalist."

"Shh!"

Rick Reed tried to point the microphone at Cora Felton, but she skillfully pushed Becky Baldwin ahead.

"Ms. Baldwin," Rick said, hastily improvising, "you just secured a dismissal in your client's case. How did you ever come up with such an unorthodox defense?"

Becky smiled. "Unorthodox is a kind assessment, Rick. Some would say bizarre."

"Let's say it, then. In all my years of courtroom reporting I have never seen such a bizarre scheme. How did you ever come up with it?"

"Easy, Rick. It was my client's idea."

Becky stepped aside and gave the stage to Cora.

"And here's Cora Felton herself! Congratulations, Miss Felton! How does it feel to have all the charges dropped?"

"Well, it beats hanging."

"Your attorney says getting on the stand was your idea. How'd you come up with such an outrageous idea?"

"What's outrageous about it? I figured out the case, I wanted to get on the stand. I saw no reason to drag this out for several days until Becky got up to bat."

"How did you figure it out?"

"As I said in court, the key was Aaron Grant. There he is, right there, trying to reassure his wife he wasn't trashing her aunt. Sherry, he's a good guy, I couldn't have solved this without him. Aaron's a good witness. If he saw Paula Martindale in the parking lot, she was there. If he didn't see Ken Jessup and Luke Haslett, they weren't. They were lying. And they weren't lying to give Paula Martindale an alibi, because Aaron Grant did that. They were lying to give themselves one. Or rather to give Ken Jessup one; I doubt if poor Luke Haslett had a clue what was going on. Which was why he had to die."

"Would you care to explain?"

"Ken Jessup needed an alibi, since he had conspired with Paula Martindale to kill her husband. They were having an affair — ah, sweet love — only Paula couldn't divorce Roger because he had a rock-solid prenup, and she wanted his money. That's a guess on the prenup, by the way, but I'll bet you a nickel. Anyway, Ken Jessup set the stage by pretending to hate her, and he sold it by refusing to alibi her at the mall. It took Luke Haslett to make that alibi stick, tying the nearly-got-run-over story to the burning of the puzzle. Of course he had no idea why. He was telling it because he was paid to, which was okay with him. Luke Haslett was a drunk who would do anything for money. All he had to do was act drunk, which was right in his wheelhouse, and vaguely remember nearly getting run down at the mall and seeing a woman in a car burning something. And he didn't even have to tell it on the stand. Just informally to the county prosecutor. Which is why he had to die."

"Why?"

"Because my lawyer's Becky Baldwin. Luke Haslett could get away with his drunk act in an informal chat with the county prosecutor, but Becky would have eaten him alive.

"So he had to die. Which worked out very nicely for the kidnappers. Because I was the only one with a motive, so of course I got credit. The killer left the Sudoku just to seal the deal. A perfectly good Sudoku, by the way, but meaningless in terms of the murder, except to tie me to it."

Cora looked directly into the camera. "And as a public service announcement: killers, for God's sake. When I kill someone, I don't leave a Sudoku with the body. Not because it would make me look guilty. Because it would make me look stupid. Killers don't sign their crimes. If they did, it would make life a lot easier for law enforcement. But most killers are smart enough to realize what a bad idea that would be."

"Miss Felton, is it true you were having an affair with the victim, Roger Martindale?"

"Don't be silly, Rick."

"You said so on the stand."

"I said a lot of things on the stand, Rick. Some of them were true." Cora made an "oops" gesture, then laughed. "I'm sure Henry Firth didn't hear me say that."

"Are you saying you *made up* the story you told on the witness stand?"

"Rick, didn't you get the memo? Henry's standing right here. I just beat a murder rap and a contempt of court citation. You think I wanna take the fall for perjury?"

Rick blinked, confused, not sure what to ask next.

"Rick, let me help you out. Everything I said on the stand was part of a carefully devised plot Becky and I hatched with Henry Firth. I am happy to say that our county prosecutor is more concerned with the administration of justice than he is with his own winning percentage. When he realized Ken Jessup was guilty, he was eager to go along. It was his skillful questioning that brought the story out in just the right way to make Ken Jessup panic and run. Thanks to Chief Harper and the Baker-haven police force, he didn't run far. But, as I'm sure you know, flight is an indication of guilt, and Henry Firth will be able to use it when he prosecutes him for the crime.

"Or should I say *crimes*. Since he's guilty of the Luke Haslett murder as well. Prosecuting him shouldn't be a problem. The way I understand it, Paula Martindale is falling all over herself to distance herself from Ken Jessup, and in all likelihood the two of them will try to pin it on each other.

"But that's Henry Firth's business, not mine," Cora said, stepping aside and giving the prosecutor the stage.

"Mr. Firth," Rick Reed said, "congratulations on a brilliant scheme. I understand Ken Jessup has been arrested for the murder. Do you think you'll have any trouble getting a conviction?"

Henry Firth smiled good-naturedly. "Well, third time's the charm, Rick."

The remark drew an appreciative laugh.

Cora tugged at Becky's arm. "Whaddya say we slip away and leave Henry in the spotlight?"

"Nice of you."

"Prudent of me," Cora said. "The fewer questions I have to answer, the better. Come on, buy you a drink."

They drove out to the Country Kitchen. On the TV over the bar Henry Firth was still holding forth.

The bartender had been watching. He looked up when they came in. "Oh, hi.

Congratulations!"

"Thanks," Cora said, "but we've had enough of Henry Firth."

"You want me to turn it off?"

"No, but we'll take a booth."

"And a scotch on the rocks," Becky said.

"And a virgin rum and Coke," Cora said.

The bartender frowned. "What's that?"

"A rum and Coke without the rum. Make it Diet."

Cora and Becky flopped down in a booth.

"How long do you think he'll talk?" Becky said.

"Hey, I tried to give you the spotlight; you wouldn't take it."

"It was your show."

"Don't sell yourself short, kid. You defended two murder suspects for the same crime and got them both off. Talk about a win-win."

"They happened to be innocent."

"Like that's a deal breaker. You know how many innocent men are on death row?"

"None that I've defended."

"I'll drink to that," Cora said, as the bartender set down the scotch and Diet Coke.

"I don't mean to be inquisitive," Becky said, "but now that you're not on TV talking in front of the prosecutor, how much of what you said on the stand was true?"

"Like what?"

"The phone call from the killer, on Roger Martindale's cell phone, telling you to go to the Dairy Queen."

"You didn't buy that?"

"You told me a very convincing story about a computer scammer from India. Was that a lie?"

"Well, let's put it this way," Cora said. "At least one of those stories was."

"I'm talking about the one you told on the stand."

"Ah, the perjury."

"Was it perjury?"

"I thought you didn't ask your clients if they're guilty."

"You're not my client. The case is over. You haven't been charged with anything."

"For which I am very grateful."

"Come on, Cora. Did you go out to the Dairy Queen?"

"Of course I did."

"You got the phone call?"

"Well, I didn't go for soft-serve ice cream."

"And the computer scammer from India was a lie?"

"I've gotten the call half a dozen times. Just not that one."

"You couldn't have told me you went to

the Dairy Queen?"

"You were planning my defense. I didn't want to clutter it up with the facts."

Becky sighed. "It's just us girls together. Can I let my hair down?"

"I thought we were doing that."

"I mean literally." Becky unpinned her hair and shook it out. It fell in blond curls from being pinned up.

"Ah, the retro look. Or is it current? I can never keep up with fashion. Anyway, it's a whole new look for you. You might consider a change of hairstyle."

"I might at that," Becky said. "A few weeks ago I was considering a change of profession."

"You don't have to worry about that now. You're famous. Retainers will start pouring in."

Becky's cell phone rang.

"See? There's your next client now."

Becky picked up the phone. "Becky Baldwin . . . Oh, hi . . . Thanks . . . She's right here."

Cora looked at her inquiringly.

"Sergeant Crowley."

Cora took the phone. "Hello?"

"Hear you didn't do this one," Crowley said.

"Well, they didn't get me for it."

"That's what matters. No one cares who's guilty. It's all about the conviction rate."

"I said something like that on TV."

"Sorry. We don't get Channel Eight."

"It didn't go national?"

"It didn't go *live* national. It'll probably make the news cycle."

"I hope they use Becky. She needs the work."

"Hey, I'm right here," Becky said.

"Too bad you're camera-shy and ugly."

"Yeah," Crowley said. "You're a TV producer trying to decide between her and Henry Firth. Whose face do you put on the screen?"

"The giant rat?" Cora said.

"Anyway, I just wanted to say how glad I am you're innocent. Now I can stop sweating the accessory after the fact, withholding evidence, and conspiring to conceal a crime charges, just for buying you a pizza."

"I wasn't gonna give you up, no matter how sweet a deal they offered me."

"Atta girl. Someone wants to say hi."

After a moment, Stephanie came on the phone. "Hey, I hear you got off by going on the stand and admitting you're a slut."

"Well, it seemed like a good idea at the time," Cora said.

"It's a brilliant tactic. Distract 'em with

sex, and then sell 'em on some dopey idea. What was yours?"

"That I didn't do it."

"Brilliant! It's a wonder more defendants don't use it. So, if you're not going to jail, why don't you swing down our way; we'll have a victory dinner."

"Sounds good," Cora said. She got off the phone, handed it back to Becky.

"Did I hear you compare me to a giant rat?" Becky said.

"I implied you looked better."

"Thanks a lot. I assume you were referring to Henry Firth as Ratface?"

"What gave it away?"

"I'm surprised. You two were so chummy on TV, I really expected you to start dating."

"He's married."

"What's your point?"

"It's hard to think of Henry Firth as a catch. And not just for his looks. I'd hate to lose him as an adversary."

"You guys worked well together."

"Once he came around. Which he wouldn't have done without your legal guidance."

"I didn't do anything," Becky said.

"You allowed us to discuss the case without violating anyone's rights. Particularly mine. Henry Firth isn't too dumb to realize that. He should be a little more cooperative the next time you two tangle."

"*I'm* not dating Henry Firth."

"I meant in court."

"I know. So, what you said to Rick Reed."

"Did I say something actionable?"

"No. About having an affair with Roger Martindale. That you'd lied about it on the stand."

"Well, I had to deflect him. Otherwise, he'd have asked the follow-up."

"Was that a lie?"

"Was what a lie? Did I lie to Rick Reed about lying on the stand? That's the same as asking if I lied on the stand."

"Yes, it is."

"That would be perjury."

"Yeah, yeah, yeah, and the whole bit," Becky said. "Have it your own way." She took a sip of scotch. "Look, I buy your whole explanation up to a point. What I don't understand is how did Paula know to frame you in the first place?"

"What do you mean?"

"Well, she framed you for having an affair with her husband. How did she know that?"

Cora sighed. "Because I'm getting old."

Becky frowned. "What?"

"I'm not as good as I think I am. Like Ratface said in his opening statement, bad luck for Paula Martindale, I'm a trained investigator. I saw her before she saw me. It sounded good and I bought it. But it isn't true. I saw Paula Martindale *and* she saw me. But she was cool enough not to let on. I don't know if she'd decided to frame me then, but this is a vicious, scheming woman, and she figured she'd get me one way or another."

"And you didn't notice her being nasty to you at the bridge table?"

"Who could tell? She's nasty to *everyone* at the bridge table. The woman has a sick, convoluted mind."

Becky was suddenly busy looking elsewhere.

Cora's eyes blazed. "Oh, is *that* how you see me?"

"It was only the word 'convoluted.' Go on. Paula knew it was you, but she didn't let on to you or her husband."

"No. She read him the riot act but claimed she didn't see anyone. Which led him to make up the whole business-meetings excuse. Which is where Ken Jessup got it. You see how it all folds back in on itself?" Cora shook her head. "I should have known the minute I saw that crossword puzzle on her coffee table."

"What?"

"The first one. When Chief Harper sent me out there. That was the first step in her elaborate frame. She tells the chief about the puzzle, which all but ensures he'll send me to talk to her. I've never been to the house, and she wants me there, sitting in the living room, leaving fingerprints and finding the puzzle. She mentions it casually, as if it wasn't that important, so no one will notice she didn't solve that one but zipped right through the next one, sending her to the mall. Did that bother you?"

"No."

"It didn't bother me, either. The second puzzle had a message on the top, telling her it was important. The end result is, once I'm accused of the crime, they all come tumbling down on me."

"How'd she know the desk clerk would identify you?"

"She didn't. I'm sure she had some backup plan. But she made damn sure he'd identify her. Walking to the elevator, watching the numbers, checking what floor it stopped on, and then not going up."

"Wait a minute. You're saying she already planned to kill her husband then?"

"Of course she had."

"How? If she just caught you at the hotel?"

"I'm sure it wasn't the first time." Cora grimaced. "That's what I mean about getting old. She followed him to the hotel, spotted me, kept quiet about it. Laid her plans. Then, when she was all set, she follows him, lets me spot her, and gives the desk clerk an eyeful.

"Which brings us to D-Day. Ken Jessup meets his buddy after work, takes him out for a drink, makes sure he has plenty, and slips him a mickey."

"Slips him a mickey?"

"Sorry. I got carried away. He plies him with alcohol and Ativan and stashes him for safekeeping, most likely in the trunk of his car. Next day he picks up Roger's car from the garage with the claim check from his wallet, correctly assuming the garage man won't notice who's taking it. He drives it home to Roger's, parks it in the driveway, walks to his car, which he's stashed nearby. He drives to the house, pulls Roger out of the trunk, which isn't hard, the poor guy's still drunk and disoriented. He wrestles him inside and hacks him up with the butcher knife Paula's conveniently left in the living room.

"He calls me on Roger's cell phone, sending me to the Dairy Queen. Of course he uses a different phone to send Aaron Grant to Walmart. Paula's waiting for Aaron to drive up, so she can scout out the perfect place to park and stage her puzzle-burning act."

Becky took a sip of scotch. "How do you know all this?"

"I don't. I'm making it up. With any luck, Henry Firth will figure it out."

"Gonna help him?"

"I don't know. After all, he did try to convict me of murder."

"Cora! You're not going to let them get away with it."

"Of course not. If Ratface has trouble, I'm sure you could point him in the right direction. It would sound better coming from an attorney than from the defendant."

Becky set down her scotch. "Cora Felton. If you start rumors about me and Henry Firth . . ."

"Wouldn't dream of it," Cora said.

"Oh, really?"

"Sure." Cora took a pull of her virgin rum and Coke. "I'm still working on the rumors about you and Aaron Grant."